SECRET

ARIES
 *(March 21 to April 19)*

Fiery and brilliant, Aries has a great sense of adventure and an aggressive pioneering spirit. Where others cringe from challenges, Aries charges full steam ahead. Like a battering ram, she can sometimes ride over other people's sensitive feelings, forgetting family and friends when too wrapped up in her own thing. But her taste for romance never dies, and a dashing knight in armour figures somewhere in every Aries life.

Alexandra's determination to become a successful rock musician leads her to adopt a disguise she may have to keep forever. But will her ambitions be thwarted when she meets Sam?

*Whatever your sun sign, you'll want to read
Zodiac, the series written in the stars.*

SERIES CREATED BY JAHNNA N. MALCOLM

ZODIAC

ARIES

SECRET IDENTITY

JAHNNA N. MALCOLM

Lions
An Imprint of HarperCollinsPublishers

First published in Lions in 1995

Lions is an imprint of CollinsChildren'sBooks,
a Division of HarperCollins*Publishers* Ltd,
77-85 Fulham Palace Road, Hammersmith, London W6 8JB

1 3 5 7 9 8 6 4 2

Copyright © Jahnna N. Malcolm 1995

The author asserts the moral right to be
identified as the author of the work

ISBN: 0 00 675044 3

Printed and bound in Great Britain by
HarperCollins Manufacturing Ltd, Glasgow.

For Laura Young

CHAPTER ONE

ARIES (March 21-April 19)
You are often misjudged as completely feisty and
Mars-ruled, but Mars was a wise warrior. They
don't call you a leader for nothing. If one
mountain pass is snowed under, the ram will
always find an alternative route.

"*O*ne, two, three, FOUR!"

The lead riff wailed from the guitar. Alexandra Sherwood picked out the melody line, stepped up to the microphone and growled out the lyrics to "White Noise". Waves of energy pounded in her veins as her band, Cinderella Complex, kicked in. They were warming up for their audition at the Cement Slab, one of the newest clubs in Seattle, and they sounded fabulous.

Roxanne Flint, her tall, red-headed drummer, slammed into the beat, and bass guitarist, Cedar Ketcham, picked up the driving rhythm, while Cedar's sister, Holly, fused in the chords on the synthesizer.

They were hot.

They were ready.

Then the sound sizzled into static and feedback. The bass blasted in way too loud.

"Cut! Cut!" Alexandra roared. "Geez. Will someone fix those levels?"

Roxanne threw down her drumsticks and stomped to the mixing board at the front of the stage. "Where's your jerk of a brother?" she snapped as she adjusted dials and knobs.

Alexandra shrugged, trying not to let Roxanne see how angry she really was at her brother. This wasn't the first time Cody had let the group down. Sometimes he could be a gigantic pain. *Why does it have to be now?* One of the best small clubs in Seattle wanted to hear Cinderella Complex, and their sound technician was missing...gone... nowhere.

"I don't know where Cody is, Roxanne," Alexandra snapped back. "But he'll get here. We've got fifteen minutes until the audition. Let's use it to practise. Not argue. OK?"

The static cleared up and Roxanne returned to her seat and picked up the beat. Alexandra tossed her long, sunbleached, blonde hair that hung past her waist. It was her signature and, when she swung her head in time to the music, it looked like corn silk spreading across her shoulders.

She smiled at her group and led them back into her favourite original song, "Illusion Lightning". Cedar pulled in the bass, and Holly chorded the melody like a pro, her keyboard fingering sliding through the intricate harmonics.

They ended up with the bass solo, and Cedar nailed it.

"Yeah!" Alexandra screamed, pumping one fist in the air. "All right! If we keep this up, we'll blow this guy away."

Cedar shook her head, her chin-length brown hair swishing across her face. "I'm not so sure. The bass levels are very funky. The harmonies sound OK, but we've got to do something about this reverb."

Alexandra threw her hands in the air. "OK, OK." She hated to admit it but they were right. Without Cody, they were just guessing about the sound. He was their expert. Their pro. They needed him. This audition was too important for them to screw up the blend. *Where is he?*

"I'll be right back. If Cliff comes, don't start without me." Alexandra set down her guitar, hopped off the stage, and hurried round the corner of the backstage area, where a payphone hung on the wall. She jabbed in a quarter, punched in the numbers, and let it ring five times.

She lived with her family in a big old

farmhouse out on Bainbridge Island, so whenever the phone rang someone had to sprint. Alexandra knew her parents weren't home, her mother had taken her father to the VA hospital in Bremerton for tests. That left her eleven-year-old sister, who would either be way up on the second floor or out in the backyard battling blackberry bushes.

"Hello?" her sister Barbara, who everyone called Bobo, answered. She sounded out of breath.

"Hey, Bobo. This is Alexandra. I'm in town. We're waiting for Cody." She couldn't keep the edge out of her voice. "Do you know where he is?"

"Um. Yeah. He zoomed outta here with Luke Henderson about a half-hour ago. I checked 'em out from my window."

"You're kidding, right? A half-hour?" Alexandra's heart sank.

" 'Fraid so. They drove off in Luke's car."

Alexandra felt the pressure squeeze tight in her chest. Her brother was screwing up their biggest chance ever in order to hang out with Luke Henderson, the biggest hood on Bainbridge Island. Luke was major bad news and Cody knew it. Everybody knew it.

"Want me to get my bike and try to find him?" Bobo asked.

Alexandra sighed. She wanted to scream and cry all at once. "No, Bobo. Our audition is in ten minutes. By the time you found him and he got to the ferry, the audition would be long over. I'd better run."

"Good luck, Zan," Bobo said.

"Thanks." Alexandra could feel her chin start to quiver. "We'll need it."

She hung up the phone and leant her forehead against the back of the receiver. Her brother had let the group down. Now she had to go back and face everyone.

Alexandra paused at the mirror nailed to the wall just offstage. With her turned-up nose and the gentle dusting of freckles across it, she definitely looked like a corn-fed farm girl. But there was something else behind the eyes, a fierce determination, that Alexandra needed to see. She took a deep breath.

"We're gonna knock this guy's socks off," she murmured to her reflection. "With or without Cody."

Alexandra hurried back into the dim club. Roxanne was standing behind her drums, her hands on her hips. "Well?"

Picking up her guitar, Alexandra swung the strap round her shoulder. "He's missing in action, gang. Maybe the ferries are late from Bainbridge."

"Yeah, right, Alexandra," Roxanne said. "It's sunny outside, the first sunny day we've had for weeks, the Sound is like glass, and the ferries are late? Right. Cody is blowing us off. Just like he did two weeks ago at the Karma Kafé. The guy's a loser."

Alexandra spun to face Roxanne over the drum kit. "He is not! He's the best sound tech in Seattle and you know it."

"What good is his amazing talent if he's never here when we need him?" Roxanne shouted. Her fair skin was flushed, her blue eyes sparked with anger.

Holly and Cedar watched the familiar scene from the side of the stage. Alexandra always seemed to be squaring off with Roxanne. Maybe it was Roxanne's red hair. Or maybe, as Holly claimed, it was because Roxanne was a Leo and prone to roaring. Well, Alexandra was an Aries with her own share of in-your-face determination.

"Listen, Roxanne. I've told you before. I'm not firing Cody. He helped make our sound what it is by going for the new equalizer and mixer."

Alexandra held Roxanne's furious gaze. Inside, Alexandra knew Roxanne resented her control of the band. Yes, she knew Roxanne was passionate about Cinderella Complex. But so were they all.

12

Ever since her twelfth Christmas, when she'd received that guitar, all Alexandra had wanted to do was play music. For six years it had been her life. In her sophomore year of high school she met Roxanne and offered her the position of drummer in her new band. Roxanne, who had been friendless up till then, had been grateful.

"Listen, Roxanne," Alexandra continued, "you may not like it, but this is my band. I started it, I front it, and I book it. I write most of the songs, I schedule rehearsals, trying to find times when we can all get together. I arrange auditions and handle the bookings. So you either like my brother, or leave. That's the way it is."

Alexandra knew Roxanne would never leave the band. It kept her sane, just like it kept all of them sane. Each one of them needed the band for different reasons.

"Would you two stop it?" Holly hissed, drawing her fingers quickly through her short, bleached-blonde hair. Three earrings twinkled in her left ear. "What if Cliff Barker came in and heard us? He'd think we were total amateurs."

At times like this, Holly, who was the group's unofficial peacemaker, usually calmed them down by spouting astrological predictions and tips from the horoscopes, but this time she hadn't even mentioned planetary transits or cosmic

13

forces. She was too freaked out by the audition.

"If Cody isn't coming, he isn't coming," she continued. "Fighting about it will *not* help. The levels are good enough. Not great, but good enough. So let's just cool it."

"All right," Roxanne said through clenched teeth. "But I think Alexandra needs to give Cody a warning. He's going to blow it for all of us."

"We'll talk about it later," Alexandra said, adjusting her guitar strap. "Remember, if we want to be winners, we have to act like winners."

The door at the back of the big room opened and they instantly snapped to attention.

A barrel-chested man stood silhouetted by the brighter lights behind him. He'd been in a conference when they'd arrived and his assistant, Mike Farrell, had told them to go ahead and set up, and Cliff would be with them in fifteen minutes.

Alexandra glanced at Roxanne, Holly, and Cedar. They nodded, adjusted their instruments, and waited while the club owner walked slowly across the vast dance floor. His skin was pale, and Alexandra could see his small, dark eyes staring at them. His jaw worked a piece of chewing gum.

He likes our look. Roxanne was in neon yellow bicycle shorts and bright green T-shirt, Holly and Cedar in hot pink bike shorts and halter tops, while Alexandra wore electric blue spandex pants with a spangled shirt. All of them had on red high-top sneakers.

Cliff Barker moved to the front of the stage and stared at them some more, his mouth working his chewing gum.

"One, two, three, four—" Alexandra counted and moved.

"Wait, wait, WAIT!" he shouted, waving his hands furiously.

Alexandra's hands slithered across the strings and a twangy chord echoed through the speakers. "What's wrong?" she asked.

"An all-girl band?" he asked. "Who are you kidding?" His voice dripped with scorn.

Alexandra exchanged confused looks with Cedar, who shrugged. "What's wrong with an all-girl band?" Alexandra said. "You got something against girls?"

Cliff's face went from white to red. "No, of course not. Hey, I love girls. But all-girl bands are a dime a dozen. Ever since the original Cranberries I've been overrun with all-girl bands swearing they can play. I can't use you."

He turned to head back to his office.

"Wait a second!" Alexandra called, slipping off her guitar and jumping off the stage. She looked him straight in the eye. "We're not just any girl band. We're musicians. Good ones. When we played at the Loading Dock on Vashon Island, they loved us."

Cliff looked at each girl in the group from head to toe, then up again. He cracked his gum. "I need something different. This same-sex band thing is a bore. I want something hot. All guy back-up, girl up front. All girl back-up, guy up front. Anything except an all-girl band!"

"You have to let us play." Alexandra's voice was tight. "You agreed to this audition."

She could feel her anger building, just under the surface, like a geyser ready to blow.

Cliff narrowed his already tiny eyes into slits. "I don't have to do anything."

"Yes, you do! What kind of a jerk are you? You get your kicks dragging us all the way from Bainbridge and then telling us you don't want to hear us? Does that make you feel powerful or something?" Her voice bounced off the back wall of the club.

Cliff's face darkened to crimson. "Who the hell do you think you are, punk? If you're not careful, I'll make sure your little band doesn't play anywhere except some dump on Vashon. Get outta my face. And outta my club."

He turned and stomped across the dance floor, his big feet slapping on the hardwood like flippers.

Silence settled over the room. Behind Alexandra, Roxanne began to take apart her drum kit. The banging and clanging grated on Alexandra's nerves.

"Nice goin', Alexandra." Roxanne slammed a cymbal into its case as Alexandra climbed back up on stage. "Now we won't ever get to play here."

Alexandra looked at her. "What do you mean?"

Roxanne snorted a laugh. "You called Barker a jerk, for one thing."

"But he is a jerk."

"I can't believe you!" Roxanne exploded. "You blew it for all of us. You and your lousy temper. No matter what we do, Cliff Barker will never let us back in here."

"Who cares?" Alexandra grabbed her guitar case and opened it. "He doesn't want musicians. We'll find somewhere that does."

"This is the hottest new club in the city, Alexandra," Roxanne reminded her. "And you just insulted the owner."

"So what? He was being totally unfair. Who wants to play for someone who makes unfair decisions based on some idiotic reason like, 'All-girl bands are a dime a dozen'." She made her voice high-pitched and tight, like she used to in

17

fifth grade when she imitated snotty Harriet Benson. "What does he know? Nothing!"

Holly slid her synthesizer into its case. "I can't believe we came all the way over here, and he wouldn't even listen to us."

Roxanne sent Holly a dark look. "And thanks to Alexandra, even if we did get a guy up front and change our names, Barker would never listen to us. Our fearless leader blew it."

A light bulb suddenly lit up in Alexandra's head. "Wanna bet?" she said, a slow smile forming on her face. "You wanna bet?"

CHAPTER TWO

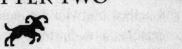

*G*one. It was gone.

Alexandra stared into her mirror. Her waist-length hair, that she had never ever cut since third grade, lay on the floor round her feet. The silver scissors felt heavy in her right hand.

Nearly a metre of shining blonde hair. Gone. She cocked her head, staring at her reflection. She looked really strange. But – more exotic, actually. Gone was the wholesome farm girl. The short cropped hair made her grey eyes look larger, her cheekbones more pronounced. But her neck looked impossibly long. And naked.

It was Friday afternoon. Alexandra had returned from the audition – or non-audition – and decided to beat Barker at his own game.

Her sister, Bobo, sat on her bed, tears glistening in her eyes. "I can't believe you cut your hair," she whispered in awe. "I mean, Zan, what if your hair was the source of all your strength?"

Alexandra grinned at her sister. For an eleven-year-old, Bobo had some pretty outrageous ideas. She and their mother were always reading astrological projections, spreading decks of tarot cards all over the house, and clutching crystals. But Bobo also got great grades, read voraciously, and helped out with the huge family garden and vegetable patch. Spring vacation for Bobo meant realigning her meridians and manifesting abundance in the vegetable garden.

"Like Samson, you mean?"

Bobo nodded. "Your horoscope says that Aries needs to avoid making any rash decisions."

Alexandra glanced at her sister in the mirror. Bobo's brown hair frizzed enthusiastically round her face. She'd inherited the fuzzy hair from their father and hated it. Alexandra had their mother's sleek blonde hair.

"Rash actions. Hmmm..." Alexandra tapped one finger against her cheek. "Maybe that means to stay out of the poison oak."

Bobo chuckled. It was good to see her laugh. Sometimes, Bobo could get too serious. "Yeah, maybe. But it also cautioned about falling victim to Aries impulsiveness."

Alexandra grabbed a comb and began flicking it through her hair. Her wrist wanted to keep going with the motion, and it felt strange to finish combing her hair so close to her head. "Don't worry about it. I'm doing the right thing."

"Can I have your hair?" Bobo collected all the long strands of hair and climbed back on to Alexandra's old iron bed. Then she tied one end tightly with a string. She secured that end of the hair to the foot of the bed, and began plaiting.

Alexandra slapped her comb on her ancient dressing-table. "Just don't use it to dust the living room or wash the car or something gross like that."

"I wouldn't do that! Besides, you know Mom and I always do the housework with the same cloths. It creates cosmic order."

Alexandra sent her a sceptical look. "OK. I believe you."

"What the hell have you done to your hair?" a voice shouted from the door of her room.

Alexandra spun round to face her nineteen-year-old brother Cody. His tall frame filled the doorway, and his dark brown eyes flashed.

"I cut it," Alexandra said defiantly.

Cody's straight nose, straight brown hair to his shoulders, and rugged jaw made him extremely handsome. But there were dark circles under his brown eyes, and his skin had the pasty look of someone who didn't get outside enough.

"Why would you do such a stupid thing?" Cody said, shaking his head in disgust.

"Why didn't you make it to the audition?" Alexandra shot back. "We were counting on you."

"Personal reasons."

"Did you really go off with Luke Henderson?" Alexandra demanded. "Luke is so low, he's practically sub-atomic."

Bobo snorted a laugh.

"Come on, Alexandra, back off," Cody said, running a hand through his hair. "I had things to do."

"You had things to do, is right," Alexandra said, turning back to look in the mirror. She flinched when she saw her reflection. It was so strange. "You let us down, Cody."

Cody met her eyes in the mirror. He seemed incredibly sad and tired. "Were the levels screwed up?"

She nodded. "The bass still isn't right. It's too heavy. Maybe it's the mixer."

Cody stretched his arms above his head to grab the door frame. He flexed his biceps. "Couldn't be. I rewired the circuits last weekend. They're clean. I'll have to check the amps. Maybe there's a glitch in one of the lines."

Alexandra shrugged, imitating his who-cares attitude. With Cody, pretending the whole world was as laid-back as he was usually paid off. Then he didn't feel pressured to get things right. *Like in school*, Alexandra thought. The teachers had all said if he could be left to work at his own pace, he'd be fine. Unfortunately, the curriculum moved at a different pace. And then there were those irritating little details like requirements and assignments. Cody had dropped out two years ago. But he could still wire, rewire, set up, and take apart anything electronic. And mix a song and make it sound like gold.

"I'll take a look at them," Cody said.

"That'd be great," Alexandra smiled. "The amps are at the Ketcham place." Her brother continued to stare at her, so she spun to face him. "What?"

"Why did you cut your hair?"

"That jerk, Cliff Barker, wouldn't even listen to us, Cody! He said all-girl bands are a dime a dozen. He wants a different look."

Cody shook his head. "You can come up with some pretty lame ideas, Alexandra, but this one takes the cake."

"I'm desperate."

"You think changing the way you look is going to fool that guy? If he doesn't want all-girl bands, cutting your hair isn't going to do any good."

"Nope. But changing my identity might. He wants a guy up front."

Bobo and Cody both stared at her. Bobo's eyes

got huge. "You mean, like in the movie *Victor Victoria*?"

Alexandra nodded. "Or *Twelfth Night* and *As You Like It*. Shakespeare's girls, Viola and Rosalind, were two of the greatest cross-dressers of all time."

"Wow," Bobo murmured.

"Only I'll be Alex," Alexandra continued. "Or just plain Al."

Cody's mouth dropped open. "You're kidding."

"No, I'm not. Listen, Cody, you know it's unfair the way girls are judged in the music business. The owners never go just with ability. It's always looks, looks, looks. It makes me sick!"

Bobo nodded her head. "At the Symphony, you audition behind a wall so the people making the decisions can't be influenced by gender or appearance."

"Where do you learn stuff like that?" Alexandra asked, impressed.

Bobo grinned. "I read."

"But appearance is a big deal in clubs," Cody protested. "You gotta look the part as well as play it."

"Well, it won't matter, because I'm going to give Barker what he wants," Alexandra replied. "I'm going to give him a guy on lead guitar. I really need that gig, Cody. We need the money."

Cody shook his head, letting his arms fall to his side. "Yeah, I hear ya. But the owners know you, Zan. Cinderella Complex has been doing really well on the islands. And since January, you've been getting some nice gigs."

"But none in town," she pointed out. "And we'll change our look. Throw out the red high-tops. Go retro-fem, you know, have the girls wear really wild dresses."

Cody smirked. "Actually, I wouldn't mind seeing Roxanne in some really sexy dress."

Alexandra shook her head in disgust. Her brother had always had a crush on Roxanne. One that would probably always be unfulfilled.

Bobo bounced on the bed. "Zan, you could wear one of those over-sized Forties suits with padded shoulders, and a slouch hat."

"Yeah." Alexandra nodded. "I could get some little round sunglasses, too. Then, if I wanted a different look, I could change to baggy waistcoats and pleated trousers." She looked down at her modest chest. "It won't be too hard for me to go as a guy, Cody."

"What about your fans?" Cody asked, his brown eyes darkening sceptically.

"We'll tell them we broke up and that Roxanne and the others have joined a new group. I'll tell people I've quit the music scene for a while to help take care of Dad. Anybody who knows me will believe that story. Maybe I'll tell everybody that Mom got me a part-time job in food service on the ferries with her."

"Yeah, right," Cody snorted.

Alexandra sent him a fierce glare. "If everyone keeps their mouths shut, it'll work."

Cody shook his head. "You think you can just change your clothes and everyone will believe you're a guy? As if being a guy just involves wearing guy clothes?"

Bobo stared at him. "Well, doesn't it?"

"What about your voice?"

"What about it?" Alexandra asked, dropping her voice lower and cutting off the ends of the words. She could tell Bobo and Cody weren't impressed. "Well, I'll practise. All right? I'm good at imitating voices. You know that."

"Yeah," Bobo chimed in. "Remember when she did that narration in the school talent show, Cody? It was so cool." She turned back to Alexandra. "You sounded like the narrator in some old movie. All ancient and profound and everything."

Alexandra grinned at Bobo. "Thank you."

"Well, I still think you're nuts." Cody ran his hands through his hair.

"And the sign of Aries is overloaded with stars," Bobo went on, ignoring Cody's comment. "Mathew Broderick, Mariah Carey, Michael Jackson, M.C. Hammer, Julian Lennon..."

"You are out of your mind," Cody said, shaking his head. "But, uh, *Alex*, if you're really serious about this – I'll see if I can pull some strings and get you another audition with Barker."

"Really? You could do that?" Alexandra flung her arms round her brother's neck and squeezed hard.

"Hey, let go."

Alexandra pulled back and looked hard into her brother's eyes. "But you'd have to be there. If only to prove to the group and Roxanne that you're not a flake."

Alexandra threw Roxanne's name in because she knew how much Roxanne's opinion mattered to Cody.

"I'll, uh, see..." he stammered.

A car horn honked at the front of the house, interrupting him. The three of them went to Alex's bedroom window. Below, in the lane that led up to their front porch, sat a faded brown and green station wagon.

"That's Luke Henderson's car," Alexandra declared, with dismay.

Cody was already heading out of the bedroom

door. "Gotta run."

Alexandra followed him to the wide hall outside her room. He hurried across the threadbare carpet towards the stairs. "Hey, Cody!"

Her brother stopped halfway down the stairs and poked his head up to look at her. "What?"

"If you were in trouble, you'd tell me, wouldn't you?"

"Yeah." He tried to smile, but his grin wobbled. He gave her a quick wave, then disappeared. Two floors below, the front door slammed.

"Be careful, Cody," she whispered to the empty hall. She headed back to her room and joined Bobo at the window. Together they watched the green station wagon bump along the rutted lane and disappear, leaving behind a thin trail of dust.

CHAPTER THREE

You have a transit Saturn aspect in your sixth house. It won't stop you from doing what you want to do, but you just have to do it with caution. Discipline. That's what Saturn wants from you.

The late April sun shone on the scrubby grass surrounding Roxanne Flint's big barn. The new "Alex" pedalled her bike along the asphalt road, squinting behind her small round sunglasses. She let go of one of the handlebars and readjusted the hat on her head. A head of short, jet black hair.

Why go halfway with the disguise? On Saturday morning she'd driven over to Winslow to buy some hair colour to dye her short hair black. Now she really looked different.

She'd decided to wear a pair of baggy trousers she'd dredged up from Cody's wardrobe and a collarless white shirt. Over it she layered a brown waistcoat. On her cropped hair she wore an old hat her grandfather had actually worn back in the '60s.

29

This is going to be tough. The girls aren't going to like it. I'm going to have to use every ounce of Aries charm to pull it off.

Roxanne's father had built his new house on the island after divorcing Roxanne's mother. The house was a huge log cabin, up-market, gorgeous, comfortable, and empty. At the back was a barn, two sheds for garden equipment, and a huge garage. Alex headed for the barn, which had become their rehearsal studio.

From inside, Alex heard Holly and Cedar working on a harmony for one of their new numbers, "Leave Me Now". It was a cool, sort of bluesy ballad with a pulsing underbeat. But the harmonies were intricate, and Holly kept messing up the bridge.

Alex parked her bike, then yanked opened the tall door.

"Hey, it sounds better than it did last week," she said, in her practised "guy" voice.

The three girls stared at her.

Confusion, surprise, shock registered on their faces. Then, recognition. "Alexandra?" Holly asked.

"What have you done to your hair?" Cedar screeched, a look of horror on her face.

"What's the big idea?" Roxanne scoffed.

Alex swept off her hat and bowed. "Meet your

new lead guitarist, Alex McQuay."

Alex had chosen her mother's maiden name as her new last name.

Holly and Cedar exchanged puzzled looks. Roxanne leaned back against the wall of the barn behind her drum kit. "You've got to be kidding."

"What?" Holly asked. "What is she talking about, Rox?"

"He'll recognize us, Alexandra," Roxanne said. "I mean, Alex."

"No, he won't. As a matter of fact, Cody has promised to set up another audition for a new band. One with a guy up front."

Cedar reached out and patted Alex's hair. "You? Be a guy? You're crazy."

"Let me get this straight." Holly crossed her arms tightly across her chest. "You're going to pretend to be a boy, and we're going to re-audition for Cliff Barker at the Cement Slab?"

Alex nodded.

"No way. He'll recognize the three of us even if he doesn't recognize you." Holly cocked her head slightly. "Which he probably won't. You really do look different."

Alex struck a pose with her hands in her pockets. "I want you guys to change your looks, too. What about retro-fem? Lots of glitz, glamour, make-up and jewellery. The works."

31

Roxanne wiggled her eyebrows. "That does sound like fun."

"Maybe for you," Cedar said, adjusting the strap on her bass. "I would look stupid."

"Listen, Barker barely looked at us," Alex insisted. "You could go in there wearing potato sacks and he wouldn't know it was Cinderella Complex. As long as we all agree to be somebody else."

"And what is this new band supposed to be called?" Roxanne asked.

"What about the Asylum Inmates?" Holly cracked, "since this is such a crazy idea."

"Let's see." Alex grabbed a tattered newspaper from the floor beside the old, worn couch. "We have to have something catchy. Sometimes bands get their inspiration from the news."

Roxanne left her drum kit to look at the paper over Alex's shoulder. "How about Anonymous Threat?"

Alex pointed to the article at the bottom of the page. "Oil Spill?"

"On Parole," Roxanne said, eyeing a photo of a man with a beard who looked as if he should still be behind bars.

Alex shook her head. "We need something that really says something about us."

"How about Fire Signs?" Holly suggested with

a shrug. "Cedar and Roxanne are Leos, I'm a Sagittarius, and you're an Aries. It's perfect."

Cedar caught Roxanne's eye. "Can you believe we're both Leos, Rox?"

Roxanne shook her head of fiery red hair. "Nope. We're total opposites."

Alex nodded. "Roxanne is a mádwoman, with an incredible drive and big temper. And no offence, Cedar, but you space out more than anybody I know. Except when you're playing bass."

Holly wiggled one hand with a wrist that was covered in bracelets. "But the ascendants and the moons make a big difference, you guys. Roxanne's got a moon in Aries, and Cedar's got hers in Cancer. Roxanne's ascendant is Scorpio."

Alex listened in amazement. Holly could relate detailed astrological information faster than anyone she knew, and she knew a fair number of people who studied astrology.

Holly gestured to Alex. "Alexandra is a true-blue Aries to the core. Aries is the first sign of the zodiac and always wants to be number one."

Cedar chuckled. "You can say that again."

"Hey, wait a minute!" Alex protested, putting her hands on her hips. "Just because I started a band—"

Holly raised her hand. "Just a second,

Alexandra. I mean Alex. It's more than that. You're aggressive, adventurous, and—" Holly leaned out and flicked Alex's hair "— impulsive. You are also able to see the weak spots in any plan."

"Except her own," Roxanne grumbled.

"And you are close to your family and friends. You're a good actor. But you can't stand deceit. Devoted. Fiery. Risk-taker. Want to hear more?"

Holly's eyes twinkled as she spoke. With her bleached blonde hair and pale blue eyes she always reminded Alex of summer sun and clear sailing.

Alex laughed. "I don't think I can stand to hear any more about me. It's too intimidating." She narrowed her eyes at Holly. "Let's talk about you, the Sagittarius."

"High-spirited, impetuous and refined," came Holly's quick reply.

Cedar snorted in derision, prompting Holly to scowl at her sister. "We can be too direct," she went on, "and are sometimes considered blunt. We have incredible intuitive powers."

"I'll say," Cedar cut in. "Holly can tell what we're thinking before we say anything. Weird."

"So what do you predict for our new group?" Alex asked quickly.

"A raging success." Holly closed her eyes and

34

waved her hand over her synthesizer as if it was a crystal ball. "I predict—" She paused, and a funny, slightly fixed expression settled on her face. "Whoa. Totally intense success," she said softly.

A ferry whistled in the distance.

Alex cocked her head. "You know, tomorrow we could catch the ferry into town and do a little shopping. Create our new look. Unless you guys have some hot dresses just lying round."

"Sorry," Holly giggled. "Fresh out."

"I don't think last year's prom dress would quite be the look we're striving for," Roxanne added.

"OK, guys." Alex clapped her hands together. "What say we hit the vintage clothing stores at Pike Place Market in the morning, and see what we can find?"

She grinned at her friends.

"And remember, from now on, I am a guy. Alex. So you have to treat me like one of the boys."

"But what about—?" Cedar stopped in mid-sentence, and blushed.

"What?" Alex prompted as they readied their instruments to begin practice.

Cedar looked at Alex. "You're not going to be able to have a boyfriend, or anything."

All of them stared at Cedar. Then Roxanne, Holly, and Cedar fixed startled looks at Alex. She felt a funny sensation of surprise.

"That's true," Roxanne whispered. "You won't be able to go on a date – ever."

Cedar frowned. "Can you do that, Alexandra?"

Alex swallowed hard. "I think so. I mean, I haven't exactly been the dating queen. I had a boyfriend when I was a sophomore and that was about it."

Holly nodded. "It's a good thing you're an Aries. An Aries can live without men better than any other sign of the zodiac."

"Live without guys," Alex repeated. "I can do that. Of course I can. Hey!" She flung her arms open wide. "I've got my music. That's all I need."

"All right!" Roxanne gave Alex a high-five.

"Besides," Alex added, "I'll be too busy to date. We're going to audition for close-minded Cliff, and blast him into orbit with our new group."

Alex burned a hot riff on her guitar to punctuate her words.

Holly answered with a flurry of notes on the synthesizer. "I've gotta give you credit for nerve, Alex. Only you would have the guts to even think about facing Barker again."

Alex grinned.

"I know what I want. And I don't plan to let anything stand in my way," she said. "We'll get a gig at the Cement Slab, if it's the last thing we do."

CHAPTER FOUR

Current aspects centre round family members or those you perceive as family. Lots of people have advice for you, but you know best. Listen to the music of your soul and follow your own vibes.

"Check out this dress, Roxanne," Holly said, holding up a sleek black dress with shoulder pads and a colourful design of teal-blue and red following the neckline.

They were at Second-Hand Rose, a vintage clothing shop in the Pike Place Market. Alex leaned against the wall, dressed in tuxedo shirt, waistcoat and baggy men's trousers. She wore a slouch hat and was doing her best to look like a guy as she watched the girls paw through the clothes racks.

Early that morning they had hopped into Holly and Cedar's truck and hurried to catch the first ferry to Seattle.

Driving by the lane that ran to the Hillslip house, they'd spotted Cody walking home. He'd flagged them down, yelled at Alex for dying her beautiful blonde hair black, told her she was crazy about three more times – then startled them all by handing her a wad of money.

"Here, Al. Go super-glitz if you want. I want you to show Barker what you're made of, too. You can pay me back when you get the gig." He'd leant into the truck and winked. "I set up an audition with Barker for next Monday."

"Already? You got us another audition?"

"Your *first* audition, Alex," Cody reminded her. "The guy thinks he's seeing a new band. Remember, this was your idea, dork-face." He tapped her on the tip of her nose with one finger. "Don't blow it."

Anxiety had filtered into her brain. Why was Cody hanging round the Hillslip place?

And how had he got the wad of money? Of course, it would come in handy. But where had it come from?

"Look, Alex." Cedar was waving her hand in front of her face. "Look at Holly and Rox."

Holly, her short platinum hair spiked into a very cool shaggy look, stood before them dressed in a sleek red velvet dress. Roxanne wore one, too, only hers was deep purple with a halter top and deep slits up the sides.

"Whoa." Alex smiled. She nodded her head like Cody did when he was impressed. "You two look fabulous."

Holly and Roxanne shimmied their hips. Roxanne mimed a drum sequence, and Alex saw that the dress, with its halter top and deep slits, would not get in her way at all.

Holly went into a keyboard imitation, bopping round the store as if she were letting fly with her solo on "Illusion Lightning".

"Yes!" Alex clapped. "Perfect. Now what about you, Cedar?"

Cedar bit her lip. "I – I don't know, Alex. That super glamour look is stupid on me. At least Roxanne and Holly have figures." Cedar glanced down at herself. She was medium height, but slight, almost skinny. She had amazing strength, though, and could wail through a gig without getting tired. But there was a wispy quality to her that might be overshadowed by Roxanne and Holly.

"OK, what about that really short velvet thing you pulled out?" Alex headed for one of the racks, and before long they'd persuaded Cedar to try on a wild magenta mini-dress.

"That's incredible, Cedar," Alex said, nodding

her approval. "You look fabulous. And the short look on one of you guys is a nice contrast. Do a bass guitar lick in it to make sure you're comfortable."

Cedar wiggled a little as if she were playing the bass part on "White Noise". The dress worked.

Then they all looked at each other and screamed.

The saleslady came running over to see what was the matter. "What's the matter, sir?"

"Sir?" Alex repeated, turning to nod at the others. She mouthed, "It works," to the rest of the girls, then turned back to the saleslady. "Nothing's the matter," she said in her deepest voice. "My, ah...sisters are just psyched." She pumped her fist in the air. "Yes!"

The next week was devoted to practising. They sounded good and, once Alex had adjusted her voice to sound more raw and intense, they all agreed – nobody could tell she was a girl.

But by Monday, Alex was beginning to feel nervous. What if she couldn't pull off her disguise? It was OK pretending in her living room or in a clothing store where the assistants barely looked at you. But singing at an audition was another matter. The focus on her would be as intense as a laser beam. And what if one of the girls slipped and called her Alexandra, or referred to her as "she". Just thinking about it made her heart thud faster.

The morning of the audition the group drove over in Holly's truck. They had felt a little silly driving on to the ferry completely decked out in their new outfits and make-up, but they had no idea if there would be anywhere for them to change.

Alex was already sweltering in her suit and tie and slouch hat.

Cedar, who was crammed next to Alex in the truck, said, "It's really hard to see you as a guy. You remind me of those guys who dress sort of in the middle. You know somewhere between male and female. Boy George. Prince. Early David Bowie."

Holly nodded. "Yeah. Very androgynous, Alex."

"Hey! That's it!" Alex cried, putting one hand to her head. "We'll call ourselves Androgynous Zone."

Roxanne gasped. "I love it."

"That'll give us lots of leeway if anyone gets too curious about me," Alex continued. "I mean, if I do something female by mistake. Which I don't plan to do, of course."

Roxanne poked one finger into Alex's shoulder.

"From this moment on you have got to walk, talk and think like a guy. Or we're sunk."

Alex gulped. "I know. I know."

As they neared the Cement Slab, Alex was worried that Cody might not turn up. He hadn't been home since Friday, except for one brief moment when he dashed into the house to get some tools, then ran out again. She hadn't seen him since.

But Cody was waiting for them. Roxanne spotted him first, standing outside the club, his shoulders hunched against the cool breeze coming off Puget Sound.

"Yo, Cody!" Roxanne called.

His face lit up when Roxanne called his name, but Alex didn't like the way her brother looked. The dark circles under his eyes were deeper than ever. *What is going on with him?*

Cody led them into the club and the set-up and sound check went by in a blur. The harsh stage lights burned into her eyes, and Alex could barely see Mike Farrell out at the front. But she could tell he was staring intently at Roxanne, a puzzled look on his face. *What if he recognizes her? We'll be toast.*

Alex was already sweating in the silk shirt and waistcoat, and her head felt hot and sticky under the funky gangster hat.

Mike shrugged his shoulders and turned away as Cliff Barker came in at the back, his big feet slapping across the parquet dance floor.

Alex felt her shoulders tense as he looked at them critically. Then he nodded slowly. "Lookin' good," the club owner boomed. "So what's your name?"

Alex adjusted her sunglasses and rumbled, "We're Androgynous Zone."

Barker shrugged. "So what have you got to show me?"

Alex grinned, then shot a glance at her band. "One, two, three, FOUR!"

She stepped up to the microphone, and belted out the opening lyric to "Hard Knocks".

Cliff Barker smiled.

CHAPTER FIVE

The Moon in Scorpio hits a vacant seventh house, so you're not likely to be too emotional today. But Venus in Cancer ticks off your cardinal planets and makes you pretty uptight intellectually. You want everything to be perfect. It can't be.

"You will suffer a disappointment."

Holly's words went round and round in Alex's head. Ever since their audition on Monday, Holly had been calling and reading Alex horoscopes over the phone. Now it was Wednesday, and the part about disappointment seemed to be coming true.

They hadn't heard one word from Cliff Barker.

He'd seemed mega-impressed with their singing. During Cedar's blistering bass solo, he had bobbed his head and even shimmied a little. A good sign. A very good sign. After the last chord had faded, he'd smiled again and given them a thumbs-up sign. Then he'd turned round and walked out.

So why hasn't he called?

Alex strummed her guitar. She was up in her bedroom, her guitar plugged into her snubnose practice amp. She'd already been for her morning run, finished her weeding chores in the vast family garden, and showered. Now it was practice time. But she didn't feel like practising. She didn't feel like doing anything. *Two whole days.* They hadn't heard anything for two whole days.

Maybe Cliff Barker was just playing round. *Getting off on power trips.* The music business was full of jerks who liked to manipulate people. The Cement Slab was hot and Barker knew it. Everybody wanted to play there.

"Be happy you got an audition," Alex told her reflection.

A bitter wave of frustration surged through her. *But I want more! I want to play at the club with my band. I want the world to hear us.*

Alex stared at her short black hair. Changing her identity had been a good idea. She was sure of it. It still felt weird to have her neck hanging out for everyone to see. There was something so obvious about the necks of people with short hair.

A door slammed somewhere downstairs, and muffled voices told her Cody had come home. It had really helped having him at the audition. The levels had been perfect. But afterwards he'd vanished again, letting them load up all of their equipment themselves. Not that they'd minded. Early on, they'd realized if they weren't willing to load and unload their own equipment, they had no business being a band.

Since Monday she had hardly seen Cody at all. He usually returned to the farmhouse in the middle of the night, or even the early morning, slept late, then disappeared again about suppertime.

"I don't want to hear a bunch of excuses, son," her father's voice carried up the stairs. "If you're going to live here you're going to have to abide by our rules."

Her father had returned from a week of tests at the hospital and was now lying on the couch. Alex had really only had a chance to call hello from the doorway. But Bobo had talked to him. She'd relayed every chore that Cody had neglected. That was what had upset her father.

Alex sighed when she heard heavy footsteps pound up the stairs and the door to Cody's bedroom slam. Ever since Cody had dropped out of school, their father had been on his case. Well, Alex secretly agreed with him. If Cody wasn't going to finish school, he'd have to help support the family. As it was, they barely made ends meet with everyone chipping in whatever money they made. Lately, Cody hadn't contributed anything.

In that case, why did he give us all that money for clothes for the band? she wondered for the hundredth time. *And where did that money come from?*

Cody's door opened again, and he ambled into her room.

"Hey, Al," he said, putting extra emphasis on the name. He flopped on to her bed on his back. "God, I'm tired."

Alex made a face at him.

"What's that for?" he demanded, a quizzical look on his face.

"Nothing, I guess. I'm just upset," she blurted out, punctuating her statement with a power chord. "I thought Cliff Barker liked us. But I haven't heard one word from the guy. We really must have blown it."

Cody put his hands over his face and groaned. "Oh, no."

"What's wrong?" she asked.

"I forgot to tell you." Cody was talking with his hands covering his face.

"Tell me what?" Fear gripped her. He knew something about the gig. *He didn't want to tell me the bad news.*

48

"You made it."

Now it was Alex's turn to look confused. "Come again?"

"You guys made it. He loved you."

"Really? Really?" Her brother nodded, and Alex threw back her head and howled like a wolf. "Oh, that is too much!"

"Wait," Cody cautioned. "I forgot to add, you're booked for the Thursday night slot at the Cement Slab."

"*What*? Thursday?" Alex leapt to her feet. "That's tomorrow! We'll never get a decent set ready in time! What a jerk. He could have called earlier—"

"He did call," Cody cut in. "Sorry, Alex. I completely spaced it. Barker called Monday night when you were at the Ketchams' place rehashing your audition for the zillioneth time."

Alex placed her guitar carefully on the stand. "You've known about this since Monday night?" Her voice hit the stratosphere. "And you spaced it?" She picked up her pillow and beat her brother as hard as she could with it. "How could you, how could you, how could you?"

Cody tried to fend off the blows from the pillow. "Hey, you've got a set all ready to go. No biggie."

"Are you crazy, Cody? Our first gig in town,

and you say it's no biggie? What is your problem?"

A flush swept over Cody's face. "I don't have a problem, Alex. Would you back off? At least you got the gig. You should be happy."

"Happy?" Alex screamed. "How can I be happy? We're not ready!"

Cody stood up and shrugged. "That's your problem."

Downstairs the phone rang.

"Cody!" Bobo's voice carried up the stairs. "It's for you."

Cody walked out of the door without a backward glance.

Alex dragged her hands through her hair. *Thursday! Tomorrow!* She had to get to Holly and Cedar, and Roxanne, right away.

A howl of pain suddenly came from downstairs. Alex reacted immediately, even before she heard Bobo shout her name.

"Alex! Come quick!"

She bolted down the stairs and rounded the corner of the downstairs hallway. Across the living room, her father was struggling to get up off the couch.

"Hang on there, Dad," she called. His face was lined with deep wrinkles, far deeper than normal. He squinted and grunted in pain as he clutched at the cushion underneath him. He twisted towards her, then he froze in surprise.

"Who are you?"

"Here, lean on me," she said, sliding her shoulder across his back and taking his weight against her. He'd been injured in a cannery accident a year ago and had been unable to work since. The conveyor belt accident had been the cannery's fault, but her father still hadn't received any compensation for his pain and suffering. He'd spent the last week at the hospital in Bremerton having treatment, and had returned home that morning.

"Do I know you?" he asked, a deep crease between his brows.

"I think so," she said, laughing.

He twisted sideways and got his balance. Her father was only forty-eight, but he moved like a ninety-year-old.

Rage suddenly filled Alex. She had to earn more money. With more money, they could afford better medical care and more physiotherapy for her father. They could even hire a lawyer and sue the aluminium off that cannery.

Her father finally made it to his feet, and he stood in the middle of the living room, gasping for breath, his face white with pain. When his face cleared, he stared closely at her. "Alex? What have you done to your hair?"

"Isn't it obvious?" She touched her head. "I cut and dyed it."

He put one hand to his back and winced. "Is this some sort of personal statement?"

She patted him on the shoulder. "Something like that." Alex didn't want to go into the whole explanation of her masquerade as a boy. She decided to wait until it truly worked, and then tell him about it.

"When you figure out what it is you're stating, will you let me know?"

"Sure thing."

He stood facing her with slumped shoulders. He smiled, but his eyes were still sad. "Thanks."

"Hey, no problem. Good thing I carry those amplifiers all the time." She flexed her muscles. "It builds the biceps, you know."

Bobo, who had been standing in the doorway, snorted. "If Cody wasn't always hanging round with Luke Henderson, he'd be able to help Daddy and you wouldn't have to worry about it."

Alex gave her father a quick look to see how he'd react to Bobo's information.

"What do you mean, Bobo?" he asked.

"He's been hanging out at the Hillslip place," Bobo replied.

"But that place is condemned." Their father

took a tentative step towards the kitchen, and sighed in relief. The back spasm had passed.

Alex stepped across the faded carpet to lay a hand on Bobo's shoulder. She didn't want the news that Cody was hanging out with the biggest hood on the island to upset their father.

"Hey, Bobo, don't worry about it. You know how spooky that place is. Maybe Cody is trying to find ghosts."

Bobo shot her a look that said, "Yeah, right!"

"Listen, if you've got your chores done, you can come upstairs and help me pick out an outfit for tomorrow night."

Bobo's eyes grew huge. "You mean you got the gig?"

Alex nodded. "One set. We got one set."

Bobo screamed and they ran up the stairs together. Behind her, Alex heard her father actually chuckle.

Half an hour later, Alex was pedalling her bike along the lane that ran through the thick trees between their farmhouse and Roxanne's house near the main road. Way off to the right, through a clearing, sat the deserted Hillslip house. Alex eyed it as she passed. White paint peeled off the outside in long strips, and the front porch sagged as if it had grown tired of doing its job. Boards covered the windows on the upper floor, and downstairs the panes along the front were broken into jagged shards backed by darkness.

A strange, empty feeling surrounded it. Even the birds stopped chirping as she rode past.

What would Cody be doing there? she wondered. A violent shiver raced up her spine as she left the house behind her, and she glanced over shoulder. It felt as if the house were watching her. As if eyes stared from behind the black windows.

She shook off the feeling as she turned into Roxanne's long, well-kept driveway. She could hear music coming from the barn.

Holly and Cedar were once again trying "Leave Me Now". It was getting better.

Alex stepped inside, her insides churning with excitement.

"Hey, Alex," Holly laughed. "I think I'm finally getting it. Next time, write a simple third or fifth, OK?"

Alex crossed the wide wooden floor. "Why be normal? Anyway, if you get it right, we can do it at the Cement Slab."

Silence.

Holly, Cedar, and Roxanne stared at her, wide-eyed.

"You mean—?" Roxanne whispered.

Alex nodded.

They screamed.

"We're on our way!" Alex cried.

"This is it!" Holly shouted. "We're in!"

"I can't believe it!" Cedar gasped.

They ran together and hugged each other. Tears rushed to Alex's eyes. The four of them had been inseparable since their sophomore year in high school. Like any group of friends they'd had their highs and lows. This was definitely a high.

CHAPTER SIX

This is probably a three-and-a-half star day with popularity at an all-time high for Aries. Be confident. Decisions made this past week are now paying off handsomely.

Thursday evening, the weather was lousy. Rain and fog shrouded the city in a soggy blanket. The group's ferry ride over from Bainbridge Island had been accompanied by Roxanne nagging Alex about Cody's absence.

"So, what if he's not there?" she demanded.

Alex and the group were seated in the big observation deck, sipping juice and watching the black sky fade into the black water. All of the nearby seats were draped with garment bags full of their clothes.

"He'll be there," Alex insisted. "I know it."

"Right. He missed practice yesterday. I know he didn't come home last night because Bobo told me so." Roxanne threw up her hands in frustration. "And now we're depending on a guy who can't be depended on. Great. That's just great."

Holly leaned across the booth and patted Roxanne on the arm. "Lighten up, Rox. He'll make it. If he doesn't? Well, we'll have to make do."

Roxanne shoved her hand away roughly. "Make do? For our first downtown gig? Like, I'm sure!" She pouted the rest of the way. Holly, Cedar and Alex pointedly tried to ignore her.

When the ferry docked, they drove the truck to the alley next to the Cement Slab. As they pulled into the parking lot, Alex was suddenly afraid that Roxanne was right. *Maybe Cody won't make it.*

They climbed out of the truck, grabbed their clothes, and were heading for the back door when a shadow slid out from the side of the alley.

"It's about time you got here," Cody's voice rumbled. "You're running late."

"Cody?" Alex breathed, grabbing his arm and giving it a squeeze. "You're here!"

"What did ya expect?"

Over his shoulder another shadow moved, separating itself from a space a little farther along the brick wall running from the club to the street. It was a man dressed in a leather jacket and new jeans. He was tall, over six feet, and, when Alex turned to look more closely at him, she caught him staring straight at her.

Shivers slid up her spine and she turned quickly back to Cody. There was something creepy about the pointed way he'd been examining her. *Like he recognized me or something.* But she had never seen him before.

Shaking off her anxiety, Alex climbed the steps into the club. *He couldn't have recognized me. No way.*

Alex opened the door. A wall of noise washed over her. Voices shouted orders, instruments twanged, and speakers and amps thudded and bumped as technicians lugged them into position.

Alex pinched herself. Soon, very soon, they'd be on stage at their very first Seattle club gig.

Mike Farrell pointed out where they were supposed to go, giving them a perplexed look. He looked ready to say something but then he was called away by a roadie from another band to set up some equipment at stage left.

Roxanne, Holly, and Cedar had quickly headed to the backstage dressing room to change. Cody joined some of the musicians from the other groups, who were standing and laughing near the wings. He waved Alex over to join them.

Alex had removed her coat and Cody eyed her suit with approval. "Good choice," he whispered. "You'd have to excavate to find any female – er –

characteristics in that thing."

"That's the idea," Alex rasped back.

Cliff Barker cruised in from the alley and stopped to give her a handshake. "Good audition, Al," he said. "You're almost exactly the look I was searching for. Uncanny. Like you read my mind, or something. But don't get too cocky. I've got bands coming out of my ears. I make no promises."

"Yeah. I get the picture," Alex rumbled in her lowest voice possible.

Barker flicked her lapels, gave her another up-and-down look, then headed into the main part of the club.

Cody and she both let out a long breath.

"Phew," Alex sighed. "He didn't recognize me. Even up close."

Cody shook his head. "I still think you're crazy to do this. If you want my advice—"

"I don't."

"Too bad. You're going to get it anyway," Cody said with a grin. "Watch the guys in the other bands. See how they move and talk and act. You could pick up a few things."

Alex put her hands on her hips and glared at him. "Like what?" she hissed.

Cody imitated her movement. He looked ridiculous. "Like how many guys do you see putting their hands on their hips?"

"Oops." Alex jammed her hands into her trouser pockets.

Cody nodded. "Yeah. And notice the way the guys tend to slouch, nod their heads, run their hands through their hair. Across their beard."

"OK, OK. I get the point." Her brother was starting to make her doubt whether she could really pull this off.

From behind Cody appeared two of the guys he'd been talking to. They nodded to her.

Cody gestured matter-of-factly to Alex. "Al, this is Bryan Cooper and Frank Peterson from Squid. They go on later tonight. Alex here's the lead for Androgynous Zone."

"Hey," they both said in unison.

"Hey," Alex said back, nodding quickly. Then she looked away to study a team of sound technicians, who were setting up some top-of-the-line PA speakers. She'd already noticed that guys tended to avoid making eye contact, so she kept darting her eyes away from the two hunks standing in front of her.

Bryan had long blond hair, with a ring in his nose and three in his ear. Frank was dark-haired and so huge that he made Alex look like the Wimp of the World.

Bryan elbowed her. "Lead guitar, right?"

Alex nodded. "Yeah. You too?"

He nodded, then mimed a guitar lick.

Frank shook his head. "Bryan is total ego."

"True," Bryan agreed cheerfully. "But what can ya do when you're great?"

Frank punched him in the stomach and they all laughed.

"So, who's the fox on drums?" Bryan asked, leaning next to Alex and giving Cody a devilish grin.

Alex blinked in surprise. "Oh, you mean Roxanne?"

"Yeah, the red-headed babe. I can't wait to see her pound those skins. Geez, she's hot."

"You're cracked," Frank said. "Now, the synth player. There's a babe."

"Holly Ketcham," Alex said, suddenly feeling very uncomfortable. Was she going to have to listen to guys drool over her friends all night?

"Watch it, you guys." Cody gestured with his thumb towards her. "Al here is very possessive of his band."

Alex punched him in the arm. Cody was enjoying this whole exchange.

Bryan looked her up and down. "That right?"

Alex ran one hand across her face as if she were rubbing her beard stubble. "I like them to concentrate on their job," she growled.

Frank grinned. "And after hours? Don't they get to go out and play, Dad?"

"That's up to them," she said with a shrug.

"D'you check out the new band?" a new voice cut in. "Just a bunch of squirrely girls."

A tall, slim guy with wire-rimmed glasses stepped from behind Bryan and Frank, slapping each one of them on the back, and giving Alex a quick once-over.

"Hey, Jason." Bryan gestured to Alex. "This is Al, their lead guitar. Maybe you should hear them play first before you pass judgment."

Jason shook his head. "I can tell already, you guys can't cut it." He chuckled after his words, but Alex could tell he was dead serious.

Alex stepped forward quickly, but Cody laid a hand on her arm. She took a quick, deep breath to calm her temper. "Prepare to eat your words, buddy."

All three boys shook their hands in mock terror. "Whoa!" Then they burst into laughter.

Cody dragged her away before Alex could really explode.

"Listen, Alex," he said fiercely as he parked her in front of the ladies room tucked in a dark corner of the backstage area. "Calm down. You're going to hear a lot of that kind of stuff here. You'll have to get used to it."

"But that guy hasn't even heard us and already he's written us off as losers. I wanted to punch him in the nose."

"Yeah, and he'd probably lay you out cold in about a second. Chill out! It's just trash talk. All the guys do it. He's trying to psych you out." Cody glanced towards the stage. "You ready? You're on after Artistic Licence. They're playing right now."

Alex listened to the guitar break from backstage. The solo sounded hot, but the rest of the band was pretty mediocre. *Guy bands can get away with mediocre. What a rip-off.*

"Yeah, I'm ready," she said. "I just need to go to the bathroom." Alex turned and pushed open the door to the ladies room. Cody grabbed her arm again and yanked her backwards.

"Hey!" Alex protested.

"Where do you think you're going?" Cody hissed.

Alex stared at him. "I said I was going to the bathroom. Let go of my arm."

Cody quickly looked over both shoulders and then whispered, "Alex, for somebody smart you sure can be stupid."

"Well, you should know," she shot back, folding her arms across her chest.

Cody put his hands on either side of her head

and turned it so she could see the sign on the door that read LADIES.

She swallowed. "Oops." Of course, she couldn't go into the ladies' room. "Does this mean I have to use the guys' bathroom? With guys in it?" Alex asked, horrified.

Cody clucked his tongue. "You really didn't think this act through very well, did you? I'll tell you what. Go in and use the guys and I'll stand guard at the door."

Alex thanked her brother, then ducked into the men's room. Actually, it looked exactly the same as the ladies' room. When she was finished, not even bothering to look in the mirror, she dashed back out.

Alex patted her brother on the back, and together they headed towards the stage to check the equipment.

Fifteen minutes later, the four members of Androgynous Zone faced the wall-to-wall crowd at the Cement Slab. Alex stepped up to the microphone. Before her swam a sea of guys, all screaming and hooting.

Concentrate, she ordered herself. *I'm a guy. I'm a guy. Start looking at the girls in the audience.*

At the signal from Cody, she counted them into "White Noise".

They flew into the piece, and Alex could feel the energy from Holly, Cedar, and Roxanne pulsing through their instruments as she sang the lead. They were psyched. When they hit the chorus, the beat was right on, and the harmonies were like molasses:

"White noise all round me,
   White noise comin' close;
White noise gets me up in the AM,
   White noise kills the ghost."

After "White Noise", they blasted into "Illusion Lightning", then did "Hard Knocks". The crowd screamed and clapped, writhing frantically on the dance floor.

They ended with a piece Alex had written the night before and they had practised exactly twice. It was called "Fooled You", and had a simple, repetitive melody with a driving bass. Alex sang with her voice an octave lower than she usually sang.

They ended, and the kids went berserk.

They took bows. Alex reached over the drum kit to pull Roxanne out from behind her equipment. Lined up on stage in their cool dresses, wearing jewellery and make-up and gigantic smiles, Alex had to admit that her "girls" looked incredible. The guys in the audience screamed louder.

They ran offstage, and Alex started to leap into Cody's arms for a celebratory hug. He held her off and stuck his hand in hers. "Good job, Al," he said gruffly. "You nailed it."

Act cool. Don't get too excited. God, being a guy is a total pain.

Roxanne, Holly, and Cedar, on the other hand, squealed and hugged each other. A crowd of fans poured backstage and surrounded them. Everyone was telling them how great they were.

"Great lead, Al," a voice said beside her. She turned to see Jason, the guy from Squid. He shrugged. "So, I was wrong. You've got one hot group."

Alex wanted to whoop in ecstasy, but she nodded and stuck out her hand in a low-five position. "All right." They slapped low-fives and high-fives, and shook hands. "Thanks," she said in her gruffest voice.

"Come on into the dressing room. Some of the other guys want to congratulate you."

"The dressing room?" Alex's eyes widened. "Oh, yeah. Right." She followed Jason into a room behind the stage and was instantly hit with a cacophony of male voices.

All round her swelled a chorus of put-downs, insults, and references to anatomical functions. About twenty guys were stuffed into a room the size of her bedroom. There was the unmistakable smell of sweat and cigarette smoke.

"Yo, Al," one of the guys called from the back of the room. "Cool sound. Great drummer."

"Thanks," she mumbled, trying not to look at the guy a metre away from her who was stripped down to his underwear.

"Hand me that T-shirt," he called to someone. A shirt came flying from behind her, and Alex glanced over her shoulder. She caught a glimpse of bare flesh before turning quickly away. A flush stole up her cheeks, and Jason gave her an odd look.

"Yeah, you really nailed that set," he said again.

Someone knocked on the door, and the guys burst out, "Let it be Roxanne. Oh, please! Please!"

Jason answered it, nodding when a voice mumbled something. "Yeah, he's in here." Jason looked at her and cocked his head to one side.

"It's for you. Talk about luck."

Alex opened the door of the dressing room.

Vaguely, from behind her, she heard the others grumbling.

"Hey, not fair."

"Some guys get all the breaks."

"What about me?"

None of it made any sense. The person who stood in front of her was a complete stranger.

CHAPTER SEVEN

"*I*'m Sam Marston." The tall, good-looking guy stuck out his hand, and Alex shook it vigorously. "Can I talk to you?"

Alex nodded, gave a quick nod to Jason, and headed out of the door. The air in the backstage area cooled her face. It felt almost fresh compared to the thick, stale air of the dressing room. She took a deep breath, and tried not to notice how broad Sam's shoulders were.

"You guys were great," Sam said. He was dressed in preppy trousers with a red-and-blue paisley waistcoat over a white, collarless shirt. His dark brown hair was pulled into a sleek ponytail.

"Thanks," she said. *I'm a guy. I'm a guy. This guy is so cute. I'm a guy. I'm a guy.*

They stood beside the dressing room where Roxanne, Holly and Cedar were changing. Alex glanced at her watch. They still had time to load up their gear and catch the last ferry back to

Bainbridge Island.

"I'm the booking agent for a club called Iron Mother."

Alex gasped. Iron Mother had been the hottest club on Second Avenue for almost a decade. While some dance clubs rose in popularity, then faded like comets, Iron Mother always sat at the centre of the club scene. They relied on big names, and some of the best bands in Seattle, like Pearl Jam and Nirvana, had got started there. Alex felt a lump the size of Mount Rainier rise in her throat. Now she understood why the guys in the dressing room had all turned green with envy.

"Iron Mother?" she choked out.

"Yeah. And I really like your band. The look is so funky. And your sound?" Sam smiled, his warm eyes lighting up in the most adorable way. Little crinkles spread out from his eyes. "I know the owners would love to hear you."

Alex gasped. "You're kidding, right?"

Sam shook his head, looked at his feet, then up again. A little furrow of perplexity appeared between his straight eyebrows, but then faded. Alex wondered if maybe she'd imagined it.

"No, I'm not kidding, Alex. I really think you would be great opening for the Veganauts on Saturday."

"The Veganauts? Open for the Veganauts? One

of the biggest bands in town?"

She couldn't help herself. She squealed.

A look of astonishment flashed across Sam's face.

"Hey, Alex," Cody called from behind her. "Quit mocking the girls. You've got to stop that. It's *mondo bizarro*."

Alex's eyes got huge, and she felt another blush wash across her cheeks. "Oh, yeah." She jammed one hand her pocket and ran the other through her hair like she'd seen the guys do a million times. "Sorry. I've been doing it so long, I forgot. They all sound like cheerleaders when they shout like that, don't they? It's so funny." She caught Cody's eye, and he jumped in.

"Yeah, Alex is a real comedian," Cody said. Alex introduced him to Sam and they shook hands.

Sam seemed relieved by Cody's explanation. "You guys picked the perfect name. Androgynous Zone. Very good. I guess you're just living up to the name, huh? Playing both sides against the middle."

"Yeah, I guess," Alex muttered, wanting to sink into the floor with embarrassmnt. *Maybe we should call ourselves the Twilight Zone. 'Cause that's how I feel.*

"Hey, Marston. What the hell are you doing

here?" Cliff Barker's gruff voice echoed through the backstage area.

Sam turned and smiled. "It's a free country, Barker. Or haven't you noticed?"

"You stay away from Androgynous Zone. They're mine. I found them, and I'm keepin' them."

Alex grinned at Cody. Had it really been a little over an hour ago that Barker was saying he couldn't make any promises?

"Is this cool, or what?" she muttered under her breath.

They were fighting over her band. *Seventh heaven*. Alex restrained herself, but the urge to scream in bliss parked right behind her teeth.

"Yeah, OK. So when are they opening for Barbed Wire? Or Broken Bridges?"

Sam named some of the better-known groups that played at the Cement Slab. Barker began to look uncomfortable. Alex held her breath.

"Well, we'll work up to that," Cliff Barker replied. "For now, I think I could manage a regular Thursday night slot."

Sam gave Alex an amused glance. "Thursday night? Don't strain yourself, Barker. I just offered Alex here a chance to open for the Veganauts at the Iron Mother. What gig do you think he'll choose?"

Francis Sprague 17/12/1926
40 Amberey Road, Weston-Super-Mare, BS23 3QL

Dr J Birkett
Dr Murdin & Partners
Tudor Lodge Surgery, 3 Nithsdale Road, Weston Super
Mare, BS23 4JP
Tel: 01934 622665

THIS IS YOUR RE-ORDER LIST-PLEASE USE IT! TICK ITEMS
REQUIRED AND ALLOW TWO WORKING DAYS FOR REQUEST TO BE
PROCESSED. ENCLOSE S.A.E FOR RETURN BY POST.

There are 6 items on this re-order form 16/09/2002

1.   FRUSEMIDE tabs 40mg. Mitte (56) tablets.
ONE EVERY MORNING
Last ordered on 08/04/2002. You may order 6 more.
----
2.   ASPIRIN disp tab 75mg. Mitte (56) tablets.
ONE EVERY DAY
Last ordered on 16/09/2002. You may order 5 more.
----
3.   CO-CODAMOL tabs 8mg+500mg. Mitte (200) tablets
ONE OR TWO FOUR TIMES A DAY WHEN REQUIRED
Last ordered on 09/09/2002. You may order 5 more.
----
4.   LISINOPRIL tabs 5mg. Mitte (56) tablets.
ONE EVERY MORNING
Last ordered on 16/09/2002. You may order 5 more.
----
5.   LISINOPRIL tabs 2.5mg. Mitte (56) tablets.
ONE EVERY MORNING
Last ordered on 16/09/2002. You may order 5 more.

Telephone requests for repeat medication are NOT
permitted. If you mislay this list, forms are availal
at reception, you can write a letter or send a fax.
Your co-operation is appreciated.

NOTES FOR PATIENTS. Read all the statements in Part 1 opposite. If any of them apply to you, on the day you hand in your prescription, you don't have to pay a prescription charge. Put a cross in the Part 1 box that applies to you, read the declaration and complete and sign Part 3. It's helpful if you can do this just before you hand in your prescription.

Not paying for this prescription? You (or your representative) should show the Pharmacist proof of why you don't have to pay, such as your benefit book, exemption or pre-payment certificate. If you cannot show proof, the Pharmacist will give you your medicine free, but the NHS may check your entitlement later.

Penalty Charges. If you (or your representative) are found to have made a wrongful claim for free prescriptions, you (and your representative) will face penalty charges and may be prosecuted under powers introduced by the Health Act 1999. Routine checks are carried out on exemption claims including some where proof may have been shown. You may be contacted in the course of such checks.

Unsure whether you should pay? You should pay for this prescription and ask for a receipt (form FP57). YOU MUST GET A RECEIPT WHEN YOU PAY THE CHARGE, YOU CANNOT GET ONE LATER. If you find you don't have to pay, you can claim your money back up to 3 months after paying. The FP57 tells you what to do.

Want help with prescription charges? Read leaflet HC11, this tells you about maternity or medical exemptions, also about getting help with prescription charges or other health costs under the NHS Low Income Scheme. You can get the leaflet from pharmacies, some doctors' surgeries and main Post Offices. Or go to www.doh.gov.uk/nhscharges/hc11.htm You can also get information about free prescriptions by ringing the Free Advice Line on 0800 91 77 711.

Not entitled to free prescriptions? Pre-pay. If you think you will have to pay for more than 5 items in 4 months or 14 items in 12 months, you may find it cheaper to buy a pre-payment certificate (a prescription "season ticket"). You can find out more by reading leaflet HC11. You can get an application form (FP95) from your health authority, some pharmacies and doctors' surgeries or main Post Offices. Or go to www.doh.gov.uk/nhscharges/fp95.htm

Using medicines. Always take the medicines you are prescribed. You should not give your medicine to anyone else (it might harm them). If you have been given a course of medicine, you should finish the course. If you have problems with your medicine, for example side effects, you should ask your GP or Pharmacist for advice.

If you are not taking the medicines you have been given, or you have lots of unused medicines in your home, please let your GP or Pharmacist know. They can advise you and make sure you are not given medicines you no longer need. You can help the NHS save millions of pounds a year by using medicines properly.

Barker flared his nostrils. "Why don't we let Al choose?"

Alex slouched a little and studied the tips of her shoes. Sweat trickled down her back. Barker was peering under her hat into her face.

"Um, I'll have to talk to the rest of the band. But it's pretty hard to pass up opening for the Veganauts."

Barker frowned heavily, the lines in his face deepening into crevices. He cocked his head to look at Alex closely. "Hey, don't I know you? I mean, haven't I seen you before?"

Alex willed herself not to blush. She jabbed her fingernails into the palms of her hands and thought about icy rivers, snow, frost, cold rain, anything to keep herself cool and impassive. "Sure. At the audition on Monday."

Barker snorted. "Nah. I mean somewhere else."

"Not unless you've been to Portland lately."

Barker scratched his head. "No, it's not Portland."

Alex cleared her throat. "Hey, well, thanks for the offer, Mr Barker, but I think Androgynous Zone will play at Iron Mother on Saturday night, and see what happens."

Sam shook her hand and Barker stormed off, his face an unbecoming shade of purple.

"You won't regret it," Sam said, clapping her on the back.

Cedar, Holly and Roxanne had emerged transformed from their dressing room, having changed from their glamorous dresses into jeans and flannel shirts.

Alex told them the news and the three girls went berserk. They hugged each other, they hugged Alex, they hugged Sam and they hugged Cody. Even Cody looked pretty excited. And the hug from Roxanne actually set him whistling.

The rain had stopped, and a very happy group loaded their equipment into the old Chevy pickup. As they piled their gear into the back of the truck, Sam watched, smiling. Alex was forced to keep up her boy charade, offering to carry all the heaviest gear. She found herself saying things like, "I'll take that, Roxanne. You just hand me the tarpaulin." Just before she got into the truck, she felt a light touch on her arm.

It was Sam, smiling down at her. "I'm really looking forward to Saturday. I hope you know how hot you sounded out there tonight. You've got a great future." He held her eyes for a minute until she looked quickly away to study a pile of trash lying in the corner of the alley. For a minute there, she could almost detect a flicker of electricity zapping between them. But that was stupid. *He knows I'm a guy.*

The girls in the truck were already pumped up. Hearing Sam's words sent them into the stratosphere. Once again they hugged each other and gave high-fives all round the cramped truck cab.

Cody was the only one who remained cautious. "Yeah, we'll believe it when we see it," he said.

Sam gestured towards Cody, who was already slouching back down the alley. "Why are roadies always such grumps?"

"Cody was born under the sign of the Crab," Alex joked. "And he really takes it to heart."

"Yeah, well..." Sam patted the bonnet of the truck. "I'll catch you guys Saturday."

Alex waved as they pulled out of the parking lot behind the Cement Slab, and Sam waved back.

They rounded the corner, and just as Alex turned to face forward again, she caught a glimpse of someone standing in the shadows, at the corner of the alley. He was watching her. The man in the leather jacket.

The truck bumped over the cobblestones in the street near the club, and soon they were speeding along First Avenue towards the ferry terminal. Holly, Cedar and Roxanne babbled excitedly about their success, sprinkling into their conversation references to all the cute guys they'd met that night.

Alex stared out of the rain-streaked window, thinking of Sam.

Cool. He was completely cool. Nice. Generous. Understanding. Very handsome. He was probably sensitive, too, and funny. *But I can stand it. I can live without him. Without anybody. Remember, an Aries female can live without men better than any other sign of the zodiac.*

Alex slumped down in the seat. *Maybe I should have that bit of astrological advice tattooed on my hand.*

She pushed Sam's image out of her mind. Another image rose to replace it. The man in the leather jacket standing in the shadow of a street corner, staring after the truck as it drove off into the night. *Who is that guy?*

CHAPTER EIGHT

Someone is not being square with you but before you rant and rave, make sure of your facts. Aries have been known to leap before they looked!

*O*n Friday morning Alex sat up in bed, suddenly frantic that she'd missed her gig at Iron Mother. She rubbed her eyes, swung her legs out of the covers, then stopped.

Oh, yeah. That's tomorrow. She shook her head, running her fingers through her short hair. Outside, a low bank of clouds hovered above the fields behind their house, where crops used to stretch as far as the eye could see. Now there lay only weeds and berry bushes.

The sticky, weblike remnants of a dream shrouded her brain. *Weird.* She'd dreamt she was playing with the Rolling Stones. Then the school principal had come up on stage and dragged her off, screaming at her because she was missing a Chemistry exam.

Alex set her feet down on the floor, wincing

when the chilly air hit her bare legs. She dived into her thick robe, then crossed to the window to check if her mother's car was gone. Her mother's shift on the ferry started at 5.15 a.m., and Alex hoped it was long past that.

The Toyota was gone. Alex sighed. Around her the house seemed strangely quiet. Her dad was probably still asleep in his downstairs bedroom, and Bobo had garden work to do every day, so she was probably up and at it. Bobo liked to get her chores done early so she could spend the rest of the day reading. There was no sound from Cody's room. *Of course.* He hadn't got in until well after her so he was probably flat out, too.

She tried really hard not to think about Sam and his offer to open for the Veganauts. How many times had they heard some promoter-type promise some great spot at a club like the Tin Can or Under the Beltway and, when she called to confirm, they'd back out. "Sorry. Looks like we're booked solid through to the year 2000. But give us a call then."

Alex started to turn from the window, but a movement at the side of the house caught her eye and she turned back.

It was Cody. *On his bicycle?* He hadn't ridden his bicycle in months. He glanced nervously over his shoulder back at the house, and Alex ducked away from the window.

Where's he going at this hour?

In a flash, Alex pulled on her jeans and a flannel shirt. She also grabbed the baseball cap with the long plait of her own hair attached and slapped it on her head. Bobo had devised a way for Alex to keep two separate identities. She'd sewn Alex's blonde plait on to a cap that covered her short black hair. That way, Bobo had explained, if Alex wanted to go to the store or do something on the island, she could wear the cap, and no one would know about her double life.

Alex appreciated Bobo's foresight. *Better safe than sorry.* And who knew when some Seattle band member might show up on the island and see her, then connect her with Androgynous Zone.

Alex squashed the cap on to her head, flicking the plait back and forth. It felt good. She jumped down the stairs, ran out of the house, pulled her bicycle from the shed beside the garden and hopped on.

In the distance far across the Sound, the skyline of Seattle rose like a paper silhouette, dark grey against the scudding clouds. *It might as well be an ocean away. And a good thing, too.* That way her masquerade was less likely to be discovered.

She pedalled quickly along the lane, thinking

again about their triumph at the Cement Slab. Her instincts told her she'd be better off sticking with Sam Marston than with Cliff Barker. But how long could she hold out against those soft brown eyes?

The lane narrowed and Alex veered into the trees. Birds chattered in the branches above her head, and at the side of the rutted lane, tall ferns dripped with moisture. She shivered.

At the end of the lane, the old Hillslip place came into view and Alex hopped off her bike. She dropped it into the bushes, then quietly skirted the weed-choked front yard. Moving close to the house, she stepped over pieces of wood, old logs, and some ancient rusted buckets, then ducked under the side window.

She hadn't seen Cody's bike, but that didn't mean anything. He'd probably stashed it behind the house. Alex knew there was an old barn at the back where the Hillslips used to keep horses. It was about fifteen metres from the back porch and, when she was younger, she and Cody used to play in it.

An eerie silence hovered round the house, and she listened intently for any sign of Cody. A light rain had begun to fall, shrouding the house in a damp, grey mist. There didn't seem to be any activity. If Cody wasn't here, where had he gone?

He'd obviously headed in this direction. And there weren't any other places for him to go except into the woods, which would be completely weird. Cody hated the woods. He said they made him claustrophobic.

Suddenly, from the window just above her head, she heard voices, muffled and angry. Alex squashed herself into a tight ball, her sneakers squishing into the damp soil. Footsteps thudded across the old wooden floors inside. Cody's voice was right above her.

"I told you, I'm out," Cody said.

"'Fraid not, buddy. Not possible."

It was Luke Henderson.

"But I told you I'd set it up, and then that's it. I'm outta here."

"Forget it, Cody. You can't just walk away from this. Not now."

Alex heard some scuffling across the wooden floor.

"Look, Luke," Cody's voice said. "You can push me round all you want, but it won't change a thing. I'm not even asking for anything. I don't want any more money – not a cent. You can even keep the equipment. Just let me out."

His voice sounded strained and frightened.

"I can't do it, and if you had any brains, you'd know that," Luke snapped.

He'd stepped closer to the window and his voice carried down to Alex clearly.

"You know too much. Besides, who can we get to replace you now? We're already behind schedule. I told them we'd have a supply by the first of next month."

Footsteps thumped across the old floorboards again as the two moved away from the window towards another room in the back of the house. Alex rose and crept forward, raising her feet over a jumble of boards and cans lying in front of her.

She stepped across a rotten board covered with moss. She still heard the muffled sounds of Luke and Cody arguing, so she leaned forward, straining to follow the voices. A drop of water from the rusted rain gutter splashed on to her neck. She reached the back of the house, squatted down again next to the wall close to the rotten wooden planks. Her foot hit something. Before she could stop it, a bucket rolled against one of the old boards.

"Wait a second," Luke's voice came from above her head. "I think I heard something."

Alex scrunched down as far as she could.

Footsteps echoed towards the front door, and, behind her, the door opened with a screech. Alex squeezed her eyes shut.

"Oh, please, don't let him see me," she prayed.

A minute later the door creaked again, and Alex heard footsteps crossing the floor back to where Cody was waiting. She let out her breath.

"Nothing. Probably some piece of this house falling off, as usual."

"That's it," Cody said. The voices were a little less clear, and Alex practically had to stick her ear to the peeling boards to hear what they were saying. "I can't take the constant panic. Every second I worry we're going to get caught."

"Hey, that's the name of the game. And you owe me money. You borrowed big time a couple of days ago. What did you do with all of it, anyway?"

Alex swallowed. *So that was where he got the money for their clothes. From Luke Henderson.*

"I'll get it back. The band is really taking off. We're going to get gigs all over town."

Luke burst out laughing.

Alex stuck her tongue out. *Jerk.* What did he know? Of course, the band was going to make it. *And I'm going to make sure our first big money goes to paying back Mr Slimeball Henderson.*

"Hey, you know your sister gives me a royal pain in the backside, but I don't see how you could go anywhere without her lead guitar," Luke said. "I can't believe you let her quit. She may be the most uptight girl I've ever met, but she sure cooks on that guitar. Man, she was the heart. Without her, you guys are lousy."

Alex grinned.

"But we haven't let her g—"

She gasped. "Oh, Cody!" she whispered. "Why did you have to open your big mouth?"

There was a pause inside, and Alex held her breath again. Maybe Luke didn't hear what Cody had said. Or maybe he didn't get the connection.

"You haven't let her go?"

Alex's stomach felt like it had just dropped into the dirt at her feet.

"That's not what I meant," Cody said, trying to cover his words.

Oh no!

Alex waited, expecting Cody to come up with some brilliant explanation for his words, but suddenly she knew he couldn't. Luke Henderson fenced stolen goods, copied pirated tapes, CDs, and software, and sold drugs. He was the master of deceit and could spot a lie a mile away.

"You haven't let her go? That means—"

She couldn't stand it. She couldn't sit there and listen while Cody let the scummiest person on the planet figure out their secret.

Bam! *Bam*! *Bam*! Alex pounded on the side of the house.

"Someone's here," she heard Luke hiss.

Alex stumbled backwards, running across the front yard and plunging down the lane where she grabbed her bike and jumped on.

How could Cody be so careless? How could he?

She heard a door slam behind her and, just as she rounded the corner into the lane leading to their house, she heard the creak-creak-creak of bicycle wheels.

Coming up behind her was Cody on his bike, pedalling hard. When he saw her, the look of fury on his face deepened to one of rage.

"What the hell are you doing here?" he thundered.

"I can't believe you told Luke Henderson our secret," she shouted. They pedalled fast round the corner and were soon out of sight of the Hillslip place.

"What were you doing? Spying on me?" he demanded. "Just mind your own business, Alex."

"The band *is* my business. And what on earth are you doing in that place, anyway? It's private property."

Cody shot her a savage look. "None of your business."

They pedalled up their lane, dodging ruts and potholes. Cody was breathing hard, and Alex noticed his face was flushed. He used to be in terrific shape, but now he never worked out. This short bicycle ride had worn him out.

"You're not stealing, are you? I remember a few years ago, Luke's brothers were caught stealing stereo stuff."

Cody shook his head. "I'm not stealing anything. That's a real no-brainer."

He rode over to the dilapidated shed at the back of their house and climbed off his bicycle. His face was covered with sweat. "Don't push me, Alex." He gave her a serious look. "The less you know, the better. The better for all of us."

Alex frowned. "What are you talking about? Please tell me you're not doing something with Luke."

Cody shrugged. "We need the money. Dad needs it. You know it as well as I do."

"But there are better ways of getting money than teaming up with that scum."

She fell in alongside him as he headed for the back porch of the house. Across the back path, Bobo was weeding the garden and she gave them a wave.

"I'm going to head over to Winslow," Cody said, hurrying up the stairs. "Do you want anything?"

Alex put her hands on her hips in disgust. "No. And you're changing the subject."

"So sue me."

He disappeared round the landing.

"Tomorrow is our gig at Iron Mother," she called after him. "Don't blow it."

Cody answered her with silence.

CHAPTER NINE

*Mercury is retrograde which can really
make you jumpy. There is a business deal in the
offing, but don't sign anything until the
retrograde is past.*

Alex's nerves felt like they had been rubbed raw
with sandpaper. Tonight they would play at Iron
Mother. In her mind Alex had gone over and over
every possibility for disaster and it practically
paralyzed her.

The rest of the band had gone over to Seattle
earlier in the day to get their hair done. Alex had
stayed behind. To help her father, she'd
explained. Actually, she couldn't face hanging
round Seattle for so many hours before the most
important gig of their life.

As she rode by herself on the ferry across
Puget Sound, her breath kept clogging in her
chest. *Panic.* By the time the boat docked and
she'd walked the several blocks to the club, her
fingers had turned to frozen sticks. She was sure

she'd blow every number.

"So, Roxanne, where've you been hiding yourself?" a gravelly male voice echoed down the hall as Alex pushed open the alley door to Iron Mother.

Two guys were talking to Roxanne and Holly backstage. Alex felt a twinge of annoyance as she noticed the girls were still in their street clothes.

Why do I have to be the one to remind them to get ready?

Then her eyes focused on the boys they were talking to, and Alex's heart skipped a beat!

It was Gabriel Stone, the lead guitarist for the Veganauts, and his drummer, Jared Franklin. Alex had had a serious crush on Gabriel Stone for as long as she could remember. There he was, right in front of her. The same rugged jaw, the same waist-length brown hair she'd admired from the dance floor at clubs all over Seattle. She'd even spent all her extra spending money last summer to see him in concert.

And there he was.

Another dream come true. She ambled over to the group, trying hard not to show too much enthusiasm. Roxanne introduced her.

Gabriel Stone gave her a quick glance. "Good to meet you. I hear you got a great band here." Gabriel Stone turned away from her to gaze once again at Roxanne, who blushed under his intense stare.

"Yeah, thanks," Alex replied. "It's time to get ready, gang," she added.

Well, this is fun. My big chance to impress Gabriel Stone, and I get to play den mother – er – father. And watch two of the coolest guys in Seattle flirt with my two best friends.

Alex shrugged. Maybe Cedar would talk to her. Where was she? Alex peered through the sound technicians and musicians crowding the backstage area and spotted Cedar talking intensely to the Veganauts' bass player, T3.

Oh, great. Alex headed for their dressing room, feeling like an extra from the movie, *The Untouchables.* She was soon joined by Roxanne, Holly and Cedar, who giggled happily.

"Wow," Roxanne sighed. "Gabriel Stone. The guy is really nice. Not anything like you'd expect."

She stripped out of her flannel shirt and jeans, and began to get dressed. Slouched in a chair tilted against the back wall, Alex watched as her band transformed themselves into glam queens.

"So, Cedar," Roxanne asked as she touched up her mascara. "What's with you and T3?"

Cedar blushed and shook her head. "He was just asking me about the lick in "Spirits in the

Material World". You know, the part just before Sting screams. He couldn't remember it."

"Yeah, right," Holly crowed, giving her sister a punch in the arm. "And he made a beeline for you to ask about some old Police tune. Give me a break. As if he couldn't figure it out for himself."

Cedar blushed again and peeled off her clothes.

"I just can't believe we're opening for the Veganauts," Roxanne gushed. "I mean, the sound techies told me they've been packing the house every Saturday since May. Very hot." She leaned closer towards the tiny mirror stuck on a side wall to apply mascara to her long lashes.

"Jared said there is this hot party happening at the Night Hawks Diner in the Market after the show," Holly added. "I guess they usually go there, and the crowd follows them. Sounds fun." She sent Alex a look.

Alex watched the three girls primping and grinning, and suddenly felt really depressed.

Holly frowned. "What's wrong, Alex. Don't you want to go? I mean, you've had a thing for Gabriel Stone ever since you were a sophomore."

Alex tilted her chair back on two legs. "I don't know. I'm just not up to it, I guess."

Roxanne stared at her. "Right, Alex. I know what's wrong. You're jealous."

"Of what?"

"Of us. We get to talk to these guys, and flirt a little, and you get to stand round and watch."

Holly tried to shush Roxanne, but Roxanne stepped across the dressing room and stared down at Alex. "That's it, isn't it? We're getting dates and invitations, and you're not."

"I couldn't care less if you dated the Veganauts and every rock musician from here to New York City, Roxanne," Alex said evenly. "I'm here to play music. If I have to dress as a guy to do it, fine."

"It isn't Alex's fault that her plan is working so well," Cedar said to Roxanne.

Alex stood up. "Don't refer to me as female, Cedar. You must be more careful."

"Sorry," Cedar said, covering her mouth. "I almost screwed up twice this evening. T3 asked about your background. I almost said 'she' lives on Bainbridge Island like the rest of us. Then I caught myself. I remembered that we're supposed to be new to the area. That you're a guy. That we know about the local scene because of some cousins." She blew out her cheeks in frustration. "This is all so complicated."

Holly put the finishing touches to her make-up. "Well, keep your head together, Cedar. Our entire future may depend on how well we can keep our stories straight."

Alex remembered how quickly Cody had slipped up with Luke on Thursday. It was so easy to do.

"Please be careful, you guys," Alex pleaded. "Practise in front of the mirror or something. Say 'he' and 'Al' over and over and over again. If anybody finds out what we're were doing, no one will ever take us seriously again."

Someone tapped on the door and Alex went to open it. Sam stood there grinning at her, his eyes twinkling happily. He was wearing dark green baggy trousers and pale yellow shirt. "Just dropped by to wish you luck."

His eyes widened when he caught sight of Roxanne, Holly, and Cedar in their splendour. "Those dresses are even better up close."

Alex swallowed her dismay. Well, what did she expect? With all that creamy skin and those lush velvets, what normal male wouldn't give them the once over?

Sam's eyes returned to her, and she gave him a little smile. At least Sam seemed to be aware that she existed. Even if he did think she was a guy, at least he acted as if she was on the planet.

"Cliff Barker's in the audience," he said, stepping into the room and shutting the door. "Who knows why. The guy is slouched in the front like a disapproving censor."

Alex jammed her hands in her pockets. "He wants to psych us out. He's tying to pull another one of his power trips on us."

Sam sent her a puzzled look. "Another? I thought you guys were from Portland."

Alex stared at the tips of her shoes. Then, she realized that Holly, Cedar, and Roxanne were staring at her, expecting her to answer.

What had she just been saying about practising until they got it right? "Uh – well – Holly and Cedar have relatives over on Bainbridge Island. They sort of filled us in on the scene, you know."

Sam gave Holly a nod. "That right?"

Holly nodded mutely, then turned away to hide her blush.

"Well, Barker is also suspicious and paranoid. So if I were you, I'd stay out of his way. Hey, Alex, have you heard The Bean Boys' latest tape?"

Alex's eyes widened. She'd been listening to "Thermal Vengeance" all day. "It's really righteous. Cool art on the cover, too." Alex let herself gaze into Sam's brown eyes for an instant and again caught that funny, sort of surprised look that she'd seen before.

"Their bass licks sound a little like Cedar's," he continued. "And the lead – well, he can't compare to you, of course. But the overall sound reminds me of you guys. Dark and fuzzy at times. And the images on that cover. Very amazing."

"Don't tell me you buy CDs according to their art, too!" Holly called from across the room. "Alex has been doing that since—" Alex sent her a quick glance. "Well, for a long time."

Sam nodded and grinned.

Alex grabbed her guitar. "I guess I'll warm up," she said, pushing past him and heading out of the door. She could feel Sam's eyes on her back as she headed out into the alley.

Behind her, she heard Cody's voice giving some instructions to another sound technician. At least he'd decided to show up.

Once outside, Alex perched on the tiny back porch jutting out from the stage door. The night had cleared and, above her, a few stars won the battle against the city lights and twinkled in the rectangle of darkness between the buildings. She leant against the door jamb and strummed a few chords.

Across the parking area, a figure moved quietly along the alley towards the street. It almost seemed that he'd gone out to the alley right in front of her, but she hadn't noticed him in the backstage area.

As he stepped into the pool of light under a street lamp, she caught sight of his face.

It looked just like the guy she'd seen in the alley outside the Cement Slab the other night. He had the same build, sort of tall but slouched, and the same slicked-back hair. Same leather jacket over a crisp white shirt, and new jeans. He looked as if he wanted to fit into the club crowd, but didn't. Not at all. He looked stiff and uncomfortable. As if he was wearing a costume that didn't quite fit.

What was he doing at Iron Mother? Alex believed in coincidence. But to see the same guy three times in the last week seemed too much to be just coincidence. But if it wasn't an accident, what was it? There was only one answer.

That guy is following us.

Alex readjusted her hat on her head. *That's ridiculous*, Alex thought as the guy disappeared back into the darkness. *Why would anyone follow us?*

Above the buildings across the street, a star twinkled. A curious sensation wiggled up her back and she looked again. It was flickering, right at her. It almost seemed as if it were signalling her.

The door opened behind Alex, and Cody nudged her on the shoulder. "Almost time, kiddo," he said.

"OK. The sound's set?"

96

Cody nodded, his face pale in the back-door light.

"You want to check it out?" he asked.

"Just for good luck. I'll be there in a minute."

He nodded, then ducked back inside. She turned back to look again at the star. It had faded a little. Yesterday, when the band was practising, Holly had insisted on reading the girls their horoscopes. Alex's had gone on and on about new doors and success and bright lights. But there'd been the usual caution. 'You love blazing new trails, and showing others there is new territory to be explored. But remember success can sometimes seem lonely. And self-sufficiency can be a signal that you don't need anybody. Watch out for giving signals that you have to be number one.'

Number one, huh.

In her mind's eye rose an image of the guys from the Veganauts buzzing round Roxanne and Holly. Then she saw the admiring look in Sam's eyes when he caught sight of them in the dressing room.

She looked down at her suit, pulling the baggy trouser legs out and flapping them back and forth. Well, she loved being a pioneer. And here she was, ready to take over the Seattle club scene dressed as a boy.

She wondered where it would lead. Alex glanced once more at the star. It twinkled, then glowed brightly for just an instant.

"Star light, star bright," Alex whispered. "Please, please. Bring me luck tonight."

Alex rose and hurried inside the club.

CHAPTER TEN

Alex pressed her mouth against the microphone. "We'll be doing an original piece for our last song."

Sweat poured off Alex's back, trickled from under her hat, down her waist, down the backs of her legs. The stage lights were cooking.

But the crowd loved them. They didn't want them to leave.

"You might be seein' us again some time soon," she laughed. She announced "Fooled You" and the band came in on the hot new bass lick that Alex had written. Cedar really hammered it, and they were off, the crowd jumping and howling like banshees.

The on-stage vibrations, from the music, the crowd energy, the lights, pumped through Alex like some kind of high-voltage generator.

Alex wailed into the mike, Cedar and Holly adding their harmonies, and the number crescendoed to the climax. They sounded the final chords, letting the reverberation echo through the club in a giant wall of sound.

Everyone was screaming now. Even Cedar, Holly, and Roxanne. They took their bows, Alex attempting to contain her excitement. *Be cool. Be cool.*

Chants of "More! More!" rang through the club as the group leapt offstage and headed to the backstage area and the dressing rooms.

A wave of kids descended upon them, patting them, shaking their hands, congratulating them. Alex pushed Cedar to get her to keep moving forward. Then the crowd gave way, and they made a run for the dressing room and closed the door on the mob.

Now, Alex could scream. And she did. Cedar, Holly and Roxanne joined in.

"That was fantastic," Holly shouted. "Totally awesome."

Roxanne's big blue eyes sparkled in excitement. "I can't believe it. They went wild."

While the girls removed their dresses, Alex changed quickly into a clean outfit. More baggy trousers, a loose white shirt and an oversized black-and-green print waistcoat. She plonked a baseball cap backwards on her hair and held out her hands. "OK?" she asked.

Holly and Cedar nodded. "Very cool."

A knock sounded on the door, and the half-dressed girls dived behind a partition.

Alex slipped on her sunglasses, cracked open the door a little to see who it was, and crossed her fingers behind her back, hoping it was Sam.

It wasn't. A girl in tattered jeans and a tight, neon yellow cropped top stood there expectantly. Her spiked hair (what there was of it, as she'd shaved two broad streaks above each ear) was platinum blonde with purple and green tips. Alex slammed the door.

"Oh, no," Alex whispered.

Holly peeked out from the partition and pulled on her jeans. "What? Who is it?"

"It's that girl from the crowd," Alex relied. "She kept waving at me and sending me drinks."

"But you don't drink anything but water," Holly said. She yanked on a snug-fitting T-shirt and a leather jacket.

Alex leaned her head against the door. "Yeah, she kept sending me water. Plain water, carbonated water, flavoured carbonated water, flavoured carbonated water from Switzerland—"

Holly laughed. "Well, she obviously thinks you're a hunk, Al." She crossed the floor and tickled Alex under the chin.

"Stop it."

Roxanne slid into her tight jeans and pulled on a sexy halter top the same colour as the dress she'd been wearing. "Better say hello, Alex," she advised. "We need all the fans we can get."

Alex wrinkled her nose. The three others gestured at her to open the door.

"Go on!" Roxanne hissed.

Deep down, she knew they were right. Girl fans could really help keep a band alive, no doubt about it. But flirting with girls would feel too bizarre. She didn't think she'd be able to keep it up for long.

Alex pulled open the door. Unfortunately the girl was still there, smiling.

Is that what I look like when I'm round Gabriel Stone?

"Hi, Alex," the girl gushed. "I sneaked backstage to see you. You were *too* fabulous!"

Alex stared at her for a long time. She was kind of cute, with a trim, athletic figure, and a bubbly smile. Something about her made Alex want to run very fast out the back door.

"My name's Candy Rapper."

Alex snorted a laugh. "You're kidding, right?"

Candy shook her head. "'Fraid not. My mom has quite a sense of humour."

"I'm glad you liked the set." Alex said, blocking the door so Candy wouldn't get the idea that she could come into the dressing room.

Candy flicked her blonde hair back over her

shoulder and gave Alex an alluring glance. *Is that supposed to mean something?* It seriously looked as if this girl was sending her "I'm available" signals.

"Well, thanks again," Alex said, trying to shut the door. Candy stuck her foot in between the door and the jamb, giving Alex another brilliant smile. "I just wanted to know, well, are you guys heading anywhere after the show? I mean, I was just curious."

Alex could hear giggling behind her. She turned and shot the group a "Cut it out!" look.

"Nah, I don't think so," Alex drawled. "I mean, we haven't decided."

"The Night Hawks Diner!" Roxanne shouted.

Candy Rapper's brown eyes sparkled. "Cool," she said, nodding. "Maybe I'll see you there." Candy turned quickly and went back out through the stage door to the alley.

That's strange. She isn't staying to listen to the Veganauts — and they're the headliners. Alex shrugged, then turned back to the dressing room.

"Why did you do that, Roxanne?" Alex demanded. The frustration of having to ignore all the cute guys and pay attention to cute girls seethed inside her.

"Listen, Alex," Roxanne said, collecting her clothes and bundling them into a garment bag, "if you want this band to be a success, you'd better court the girl fans. You know how loyal they are. You don't have to date them – I just think it would be a good idea to let them know you're available."

"But I'm not!"

She shrugged. "You know I'm right. No lead singer turns his back on his fans."

Alex jammed her hands into her pockets and slumped against the wall. Beside her, the mirror reflected her glum face. Her skin was pale, and under the backwards baseball cap, her hair stuck out in little black tufts. She looked like a pouting schoolboy who'd just been put in detention.

Suddenly Cody's face came swimming in behind her, and he caught her eye in the reflection. "I guess playing a boy is a lot more complicated than just cutting your hair and wearing suits. Regrets?"

A knock sounded on the door, and she frantically shook her head at Roxanne. She didn't want to talk to Candy Rapper again. She just didn't want to deal with any more girl fans.

"Oh, hi. Yeah. Come on in," Roxanne cooed.

When Alex turned round, she let out a long breath of relief. It was Sam, grinning from ear to ear. He bounced a little and snapped his fingers. Alex laughed in spite of her sour mood. "What are you so jazzed about?" she asked.

"I am the bearer of good – and I mean *good* – news. The management thinks you are volcanic. Way beyond hot. We want to book you for a limited engagement."

Holly, Cedar and Roxanne screamed.

Alex grabbed Cody's hand, their eyes locking in similar expressions of happiness. "No regrets, Cody," she murmured. "No regrets."

"Listen, before you guys leave tonight," Sam continued, "I need a verbal agreement that Androgynous Zone won't play anywhere else for the duration of the engagement."

"No problem," Alex said on behalf of them all.

Sam bobbed his head happily. "Good, good. We'll have the contract drawn up tomorrow. Oh. I almost forgot. You guys OK for a photo shoot next week sometime? We need to get some promotional pictures of you. We intend to do a full publicity blitz – press releases, print and radio ads, posters, the works."

"Are you kidding?" Roxanne gushed. "That's fantastic."

"By the way, Cliff Barker came running up to me asking what I knew about your background. The guy is turning into a psycho. He insists there's something weird about you." Sam laughed, and Alex noticed that when he was really amused by something, his smile deepened and a dimple appeared in his right cheek. "If you've got Barker guessing," Sam said, "you're really on your way."

They loaded their clothes into the truck and then returned to the club to hear the Veganauts. Alex figured she'd probably seen the 'Nauts play at least eight times. But this time was different. Gabriel Stone not only mentioned Alex and the girls by name, but he gave Androgynous Zone his stamp of approval. Alex was now a peer listening to her new friends play. It was the experience she'd dreamed of.

Afterwards, Androgynous Zone joined the Veganauts at the Night Hawks Diner, a Fifties funk palace of greasy cheeseburgers and fries, and fifty-year-old waitresses who called you "honey". The owners had recently opened up the back wall and added a pool room, which had only increased the diner's popularity.

Gabriel and Jared were hanging out with Roxanne and Holly, while T3 and Cedar continued their discussion of classic bass riffs over slices of pizza. Now and then, Gabriel would argue a point of music with T3, and they'd shout at each other. Then they'd burst out laughing. Alex admired their easy camaraderie.

Candy Rapper hadn't shown up, and Alex felt a little of the nervous tension ease from her shoulders. She chatted with some of the regulars who'd seen the show, wolfed down a hamburger and was about to head out of the front door when Sam walked in.

He waved to the girls and to the Veganauts, then headed straight for her.

"Hey, Alex, I'm glad you're still here. I wanted to talk some more about the show tonight. But I had to finish my shift first and hand the place over to the real night owls."

His dimple peeked out of his cheek at her, and she felt the sizzle of energy she promised herself she was going to ignore.

"So you get the early shift?" she asked.

He nodded. "I'm on until one, usually. Now and then, if the place seems short-handed, I'll stick round, but I'm not really the all-nighter type." Sam signalled for a waiter to bring him coffee, then collected his cup and headed for the pool room.

Alex found herself following him. "If you don't like staying up late, what are you doing in the music business?"

He chuckled. "I guess I'm sort of a freak. I love the business end of it. Organizing the bands, setting up photo shoots, promotion, working up the contracts. Let me tell you, among musicians, someone who likes that stuff is rare."

"Boy, tell me about it," she said, carefully modulating her voice so it sounded low and gravelly. "I have to book the gigs, and set up rehearsals for the Zone. Plus do our arrangements and write the songs. I mean, sometimes it's really fun, but much of the time it's a lot of work."

Sam gave her an admiring look as he chalked his pool cue. "A lot of bands could use your kind of talent, let me tell you. Some of the guys are – well – flaky. To say the least."

Sam grabbed the triangular frame, positioned the balls inside it, and slid it across the table. He peered over his shoulder at her. "You play?"

Alex grinned. "Yeah, I do."

"Come on. I'll let you break."

Alex plucked a cue from the wall-rack, felt its weight, put it back, and grabbed another one. She set it on the felt tabletop and rolled it slightly, to see how straight it was.

Sam watched her closely. "Uh-oh. Why do I get the feeling I'm playing with a ringer?"

Alex grinned but said nothing. She leant over the end of the table, aimed the cue, and shot her break. The balls obediently scattered into position, the 3-ball dropping softly into the right corner pocket.

Alex laughed at Sam's expression of dismay.

"Look out, Sam," Roxanne called from the

booth she and Holly shared with Gabriel and Jared. "You're playing with a shark." Gabriel and Jared nodded to Alex, and Gabriel gave her the thumbs up. Then he and Jared went back to lavishing attention on her band.

Alex was amazed to discover she didn't feel a single pang of jealousy.

Let them have the Veganauts. I'm here with Sam.

"12 ball, in the left side pocket," Sam called. He missed and Alex shrugged, trying to make sure he knew that this was a friendly game. The last thing she wanted to do was compete with him.

She called a shot and scratched. Not on purpose. Her backspin misfired and the cue ball went rolling backwards right into the side pocket.

Sam grinned and nodded. "Hey, too bad." Sam's eyes twinkled at her again, and the dimple appeared. He positioned himself to try a tricky bank shot off the right rail.

Alex held her breath. She actually wanted him to make it.

He made the shot with ease, and Alex realized Sam was a very good player. Alex felt the tight, thrumming beat of excitement in her blood. The excitement of a good game, one that challenged her skill.

"I can't tell you how glad I am Androgynous

Zone finally made it to Seattle," Sam said as he lined up a particularly difficult shot. Two of their balls were "frozen", sitting side by side right in front of the left side pocket. He needed to bump his in and make sure hers stayed out.

"Yeah, me, too," she said, watching him angle his lean body along the right rail. He was graceful, muscular and controlled.

He aimed, and his striped ball edged towards the pocket and disappeared. He'd not only made his shot, but he'd landed her ball in an impossible position.

She caught his eye and grinned in appreciation. "Marston, you're nasty, you know that?"

"Nasty is mild compared to the names I've been called," he replied.

Alex contemplated her shot. She had two balls on the table, and he had one. If she came at her shot from the end of the table, she'd have to bend way over the rail. She tried out the position. In the mirror on the left wall of the pool room, she caught a glimpse of Sam letting his eyes move down her body appraisingly. Catching himself, he turned away, his face bright red. She backed off the table.

This is too weird.

They were supposed to be two guys enjoying a game of pool. But whenever Alex got close to him to check out a shot, a zap of electricity came zinging at her, and she backed away.

Concentrate. A backspin on number 7 should do it.

Alex shot, and the cue ball did exactly what it was supposed to, bumping the 7-ball to the end rail. It caromed back, tapped the 1 into the bottom left corner, then landed in the side pocket.

Sam let out a breath. "What a shot!" he crowed. "That was amazing." He paused and gave her one of his serious stares. "You're incredible, you know that?"

He stuck out his hand to shake hers. Both of their palms were warm.

Alex withdrew her hand quickly. *I'd better get out of here before I do something stupid like throw my arms round his neck.*

"You up for another game?" Sam asked.

"Nah. I gotta go." Alex poked her cue back into the rack. Her cheeks were flushed. She spun in a circle, looking for a place to hide and regain her cool. There wasn't any place except the ladies room. *And I can't go there.*

"Well, OK." Sam really sounded disappointed. Part of Alex rejoiced. But the other part, the guilty part, felt miserable because nothing could ever come of this relationship.

"I'll call you," he said, suddenly sounding

businesslike. "And we'll go over the contract for your gig at Iron Mother."

"Cool." Alex nodded bruskly, then pulled her cap round frontwards and shoved it down over her forehead. "Catch you later, then."

"Sure."

As she hurried down the street to the ferry terminal, the lyrics of her song, "Fooled You", went round and round in her head:

"Fooled you.
Didn't I tell you not to trust me?
Fooled you.
Didn't I tell you not to try?
  The game is more important,
  The game is worth the lie.
So I fooled you without blinking.
Now it's time to say goodbye."

CHAPTER ELEVEN

"*F*or the best view of the Seattle skyline, please go to the observation deck."

The recorded announcement crackled through the boat's loudspeakers above Alex's head. She ignored it. This was the 2.20 a.m. ferry, and few of the passengers in the lounge took the announcer up on her offer. Alex slumped down in the vinyl seat, propped her feet on the railing, and gazed through the huge glass windows at the murky waters of Puget Sound.

Her rousing pool game with Sam had plunged her into a depression she couldn't seem to shake. Sam seemed to really like her. As a friend, of course. She knew she liked him. There was a nice relaxed feeling when they were together. Nothing false or manufactured. Except for not being what she said she was.

I might as well forget him. He'll never speak to me again if he finds I've been lying to him.

Alex's eyes grew heavy as she stared at the churning water outside. Sitting up quickly, she shook her head.

I need a cup of coffee.

Stumbling out of the soft padded seat, she headed for the coffee machine in the concession area on the upper deck, where her mother worked the day shift.

Alex poured herself a cup of muddy sludge, then wandered outside on the deck to take a shortcut down the service stairs to the observation lounge. As she went round a corner, she ran smack into someone coming out of the lounge.

Gasping, she held her coffee out to prevent the sloshing liquid from ruining her clothes.

"Gosh, I'm sorry, Alex," a girl giggled. "I didn't mean to cause a collision. But I'm sure glad I found you."

Alex felt weak. In front of her stood Candy Rapper, her white blonde hair still standing straight up. Her heavily made up eyes sparkled in unabashed adoration.

"Candy. What are you doing here?" Alex cried, nearly forgetting to use her guy voice. "It's two-thirty in the morning."

"I was looking for you." Candy said, fluttering her lashes.

Alex frowned. "But how'd you know I'd be on the ferry."

"You told, me silly," Candy gushed. "Don't

you remember?"

"No." Alex was absolutely certain that she had told Candy nothing about her personal life. So how did Candy know she'd be taking the ferry home? *She must be following me everywhere I go.*

Alex had an overwhelming desire to get away from this girl. But Roxanne's voice, reminding her to be nice to the female fans, played over in her head. "Um, Candy. It's good to see you," Alex said, roughly. "But I gotta run. Maybe I'll see you at the gig next week at Iron Mother."

"Alex – wait!" Candy called.

But Alex was too fast for her. Chucking her coffee in a huge trash barrel chained to the wall, Alex bolted down the passageway towards the doors leading to the parking bays beneath the main deck. Footsteps pounded along the corridor behind her.

Alex opened the first door she came to and dashed inside, swerving along the first row of parked cars.

The door to the parking area creaked open, and Alex ducked down.

"Alex!" Candy called in a sweet voice. "You know you can't get away from me."

Wanna bet?

Alex slid round to the opposite side of one of the cars parked at the very back of the parking bay. Silently, she tried one of the back doors and smiled when it opened. She crawled inside, pulled the door shut, and crouched down, wrinkling her nose at the musty smell of the car floor. She sat shrouded in darkness and waited. The window above her was open a crack so she could hear, but the sound was muffled. Her legs began to cramp, and all she could hear was her own heartbeat pounding in her ears.

In a few moments, footsteps approached. They paused.

Don't stop. Keep moving.

Alex squeezed her eyes shut. Ever since she had been a kid, whenever she was hiding, she had convinced herself that closing her eyes made her harder to find.

Well, it can't hurt.

Finally the footsteps moved on, clanging up the metal stairs. The door swung shut behind them.

Alex let out a long breath, then slowly peered up over the edge of the window, hoping she wouldn't come face to face with a blonde maniac.

Nobody was there.

She uncurled herself from her hiding place, then once out of the car, stretched out the kinks in her legs. She dug into her duffel bag that she had slung over her shoulder and pulled out her baseball cap with the plait and a very feminine flowered dress, a pair of clogs and some printed tights. Alex quickly tugged off her waistcoat and trousers and stuffed them in the bag. Having put on dress, tights and clogs, she pulled on her cap and flipped her long plait back and forth to check it. She found some mascara rolling round the bottom of the duffel bag along with some bright red lipstick. She ducked down in front of the wing mirror of a pick-up and quickly applied some make-up. "Presto Change-o. "But just to be on the safe side..."

Keeping a wary eye for Candy, she headed for the service door at the back of the parking area. She ran down a damp corridor and pulled open a faded yellow door marked PRIVATE.

Only one person was inside, and Alex sighed when she saw him.

"Hey, Mike. I need your help."

Mike Sandusky had worked the ferries for fifteen years. He could do just about anything, from rewiring the lights to repairing the devices that controlled the loading ramps. Right now, he was sitting with his feet propped on the back of the chair in front of him, reading a back issue of *Rolling Stone*.

"Anything, Alexandra. You know I live to serve you." His voice was permanently hoarse because he had once been in a rock band and had damaged his vocal chords. He'd always had a soft spot for Alex and her musical aspirations.

"Yeah, right. I'm having a bit of a problem."

Mike's hazel eyes turned dark. "Boyfriend? Just show him to me. I'll take care of him." He jumped out of his chair and tossed down the magazine. "What do you want? I should maybe punch him for you? Maybe toss him overboard?"

Alex laughed. "No, no. There's this fan who's bugging me."

"Where is he? I'll strap him to a chair. Revoke his ferry pass. Make him drink a gallon of that crankcase fluid they call coffee."

"No. It's – well – it's a little hard to explain. It's not a guy."

Mike's eyes narrowed. "It's not a guy?"

She shook her head.

"You're being followed by a girl fan? That's very weird, Alex. I mean – I didn't know—" He blushed.

"No, no, it's not like that." This was going to be harder than she thought. The only way she would be able to get Mike to help her was to tell him the whole story, and hope he could keep a secret.

"You see, I'm disguising myself as a boy." She pulled off the baseball cap and ruffled her hair to show him the difference in her appearance. "Why? Because this club owner in Seattle wouldn't even listen to my band unless we were something other than an all-girl band. Then this other club hired us and we're doing great. So here I am. Stuck as a boy."

Mike studied her sceptically. "A boy, huh? I guess wanting to hit it big can make people do strange stuff."

"Will you help me?" Alex pleaded.

"What do you want me to do?"

"Could you maybe hide me?"

Mike furrowed his brow and looked round the grungy lounge. "You probably shouldn't stay in here. Crew members check in and out of here all night during their breaks." He thought for a moment, putting his finger on his lips. "There's a storage cupboard on this deck. It's pretty big."

"A cupboard? Uh, I don't know, Mike. The idea of hiding in a cupboard doesn't really appeal to me."

"Hey, it's only for a few minutes. We're almost to the slip at Winslow."

Outside in the corridor, footsteps approached and hesitated. Alex had a sickening feeling it was Candy.

"OK, I'll take the cupboard," she decided.

Mike nodded. "I'll let you ride in the utility

truck when we dock. That way this groupie won't see you drive off either."

Alex grinned at Mike. "Thanks."

Mike opened the door to the corridor, peered left and right, then signalled for Alex to follow him. The storage cupboard ended up being almost as big as her bedroom at home. Cables, wires and pulleys lined one wall. On another wall hung fat coils of rope. Extra chairs for the lounge, spare tables for the coffee shop, and a broken espresso machine were stacked up off to one side. Alex settled herself into one of the black imitation leather chairs and curled up. A musty, wet smell filled the air.

Mike nodded at her and gave her a thumbs-up sign. "I'll lock you in. You should be OK. Like I said, it's just for a few more minutes."

She had barely got comfortable, her legs tucked under her, when Mike returned. "We're pulling in. Might as well climb in the truck. Listen, does that girl have white blonde hair that looks like it's been dipped in paint? And is she wearing jeans and a yellow top?"

"Yeah," Alex said. "That's our girl."

"She's been crawling all over the boat. Persistent little thing, ain't she?"

Mike led Alex to his truck, she climbed in and he shut the door.

"Excuse the mess." He pushed aside a pile of empty burger wrappers and paper coffee cups as he got into the driver's seat.

"That's OK, Mike. I really appreciate this, you know."

Repair trucks were usually the first to leave, so they didn't have long to wait before Alex heard the clunking and thumping of the ferry docking at the pier. She ducked down as they passed a row of cars, and then, as they bounced on to the ramp, she risked a peek over the side of the window.

Candy Rapper stood on the pier, her hands on her hips, a perplexed look on her face. She was carefully checking each car as it pulled off the ferry.

"Geez, I can't believe her," Alex gasped.

Mike dropped Alex at the bottom of the lane that led to her farmhouse.

"Thanks again, Mike!" she called as she jumped down from the truck.

He waved. "No problem. You stay away from that girl, Alexandra. She looked a little whacko to me." He chuckled as he pulled away, and Alex headed down the lane towards her house. It was pitch black, and rustlings and stirrings in the undergrowth bordering the path made her quicken her steps.

She was soon at the farmhouse, but she

hesitated when she caught sight of movement on the front porch.

Who could be up at this hour? As she drew closer, Alex recognized the silhouette of a guy seated on the porch swing.

Luke Henderson.

"Alex," he said in his perpetually bored voice. "Finally."

"What are you doing here?" Alex whispered, peering at him through the darkness.

Luke evaded her question. "I hear the band was a hit."

"I'm not with the—"

Luke raised one hand. "Don't bother to lie to me. Cody told me all about your masquerade."

Alex stepped up on to the porch and perched on the edge of a worn-out wicker chair. She wanted to go to bed. "What is it you want, Luke? There must be some reason you're camping out on our porch at three in the morning."

"I just wanted to ask you to do me a favour," he said, flashing his killer, Jack Nicholson smile.

"Now why would I want to do you a favour?" Alex sent him a disgusted look.

"Because you care about your brother," he said softly.

Fear coiled inside Alex.

"What is that supposed to mean?" she asked,

trying to sound nonchalant.

"We have a little business deal going, and Cody wants to drop the ball. I just think you should persuade him to stick with it."

Alex shook her head. "The last thing I'd do is tell him to stick with you."

"Don't be so hasty, Alex." An edge of irritation crept into his smooth voice. "I know your little secret, remember?"

Alex felt a flicker of alarm. "You wouldn't."

"Oh, yes, I would. One phone call would be all it takes. And your so-called music career would be over before it even got started. Think of the humiliation when everybody in town finds out you can't get a gig unless you dress like a guy."

Luke had her. Androgynous Zone was just getting a name. If word got out, they'd be laughed out of the club scene.

Alex took a deep breath. "If you want me to help you, you better tell me what this so-called business is." Alex thought of all the things Luke could conceivably be mixed up in that might be the least dangerous.

Luke laughed. "The less you know, the better. Just talk to him, OK? You can be very convincing when you want to be, Alex."

Luke reached his hand out to touch her arm and she slapped it away. "Keep your paws off me,

Luke. Anything to do with you is a huge mistake."

Luke rose, easing his tall body out of the creaky swing. "The biggest mistake of Cody's life would be to back out now. And your musical career depends on how well you convince him of that. Remember that, Alex."

Luke turned his back on her and headed down the dark lane, his hands stuffed into his pockets.

Alex had a sinking feeling that whatever Cody was up to was much worse than she could ever imagine.

"Oh, Cody," she whispered into the black night. "What have you done?"

CHAPTER TWELVE

*You have romance on the brain and it's in
opposition to your ninth house squaring that
Neptune in your sixth house of work. You want
both love and success. You're not going
to have both.*

Alex glanced down at the handwritten list in her hand.

Buy new strings for Cedar's bass. Pick up my suits at the cleaners. Buy new clothes. Photo shoot.

Photo shoot.

She still couldn't quite believe that Sam had actually booked them into a photo session with one of the best photographers in the city, Edward Ventriss. His grainy, in-your-face photos of some of the best West Coast bands had made the covers of *Rolling Stone* and *Spin*. When Sam had called Alex to let her know that's who would be photographing them, she had freaked out.

"Why? Why is Ventriss agreeing to shoot us?"

Alex shouted into the phone. "We're nobody."

"Yeah, I know it's unusual. I mean, he's the best, isn't he? But he owes me a couple of favours," Sam had said. "That's OK, isn't it?"

"OK? It's fabulous!" Alex's voice had started to hit the stratosphere and she quickly lowered it. "It's just unbelievable."

That was a week ago. Now Alex was in her bedroom, getting ready to go to the Edward Ventriss studio.

A newspaper crinkled across the room and Alex looked at her sister who was sitting cross-legged on the bed, eating a jam doughnut while she read the latest issue of *The Rocket*, the hippest journal on music and events in Seattle.

"It says here," Bobo said, "and I quote, 'Androgynous Zone is the hottest new arrival on the music scene. Supported by a taut rhythm section, and fuelled by raw passion, the Zone pounds out song after song with a furious energy that is infectious and irresistible. But the key to the band's meteoric rise is Alex McQuay—'" Bobo raised her head. "McQuay?"

Alex shrugged. "I had to change my last name, so I took Mom's maiden name."

"Oh." Bobo took a big bite of doughnut and some red jam squished out on to her chin. She didn't seem to notice. "'Alex McQuay, who soars to new heights as lead singer and guitarist. His songs, replete with clever hooks and teasing, elliptical lyrics, are already on a par with the best round the Sound. Coupled with a guitar style that can only be described as masterful—'"

Alex's eyes got big. "It says that? Where?" Alex hopped off her bed and grabbed the paper out of Bobo's hand.

There was a full column review of the bands at Iron Mother, and Androgynous Zone got the largest mention. "'A howling sensation, combined with a deceptively creamy presentation. Something totally different, definitely *THE* band to watch,'" she read. "Whoa, that is so cool."

"I can't believe my sister is a rock star," Bobo gushed. "Or I guess I should say, brother. What are you?"

Alex, who was rereading the column, raised her head. "Good question."

"What time is your photo session?" Bobo asked, licking the powdered sugar off her fingertips.

"Two o'clock. Then afterwards, Sam and I might shoot some pool."

Bobo paused in mid-lick. "A date?"

Alex shook her head. "Bobo, Sam thinks I'm a guy."

Bobo squinted at her sister. "And you'd like

him to think you're a girl."

Alex nodded wistfully. "Now I know how spies feel. Always pretending to be someone else. It's not fun."

"And Roxanne, Holly and Cedar get to go out and have a good time, right?"

Alex flopped back on the bed. "Roxanne and Holly have been dating everybody in Seattle."

"Slight exaggeration?" Bobo asked, raising one eyebrow. For an eleven-year-old she was pretty astute.

"Only slight, let me tell you," Alex replied. She raised herself up on one elbow. "You know, Bobo, it's weird. I can get totally into being a boy on stage. No problem. It's like a role, you know. Actors do it every day. But offstage?" She plucked at the threads on her bedspread. "It's like I don't know who I am any more."

Bobo got off her bed and patted Alex on the head. "Don't worry, Zan. Things will get better. Success and happiness are in your chart."

Three hours later, Alex stumbled towards the large red-brick warehouse, her arms full of packages. She was out of breath from running three blocks. She'd had to wait for her clothes to be finished at the cleaners, and she was twenty minutes late.

Alex rounded the corner to the front entrance,

then skidded to a stop. Candy Rapper was outside the front of the studio, leaning against a gigantic slab of concrete, filing her nails.

Geez, that girl never gives up!

Candy had been at every show at Iron Mother, always standing right in the front and waving to Alex, even going so far as to blow kisses. It was nauseating.

Alex turned round and headed down the back alley. She glanced over her shoulder once to make sure Candy wasn't following her.

Ker-thud!

She slammed into a tall, immovable body parked in front of her. Alex's packages flew out of her hands, and a rough, steadying grip on her arm kept her from falling.

"Whoa! Slow down," Sam said. "Are you being chased by the cops, or what?"

Alex let out a breath. "No, it's worse than that. There's a girl following me."

"That blonde?"

"Yeah. She's like a fungus. She won't go away."

"Come with me." Sam led her to a door, cut deep in the wall. Half-obscured by a pile of soggy cardboard boxes and stained wooden crates, it was almost impossible to see.

They slipped inside the door, and Alex let out

another sigh of relief. It was moments like these that Alex found her impulse to gush almost overwhelming. Not that she was a gushy person. But something about Sam made her want to thank him more profusely than maybe a boy would. She clamped her teeth together, and went into her hey-it's-cool mode.

"Thanks," she said, hurrying along the dimly lit hallway towards a service elevator. "Most bands have hordes of fans. I just have one super sticky one."

Sam smiled. "Are you kidding? You're packing the club. Even when you're not playing, kids are always asking about you. Don't worry. You've got plenty of fans. By the way, I brought you a tape."

As he stepped into the elevator, he handed her a plastic case with a cassette inside.

"What's this?"

"A new group from Anchorage. Thought you'd like to hear them. They gig here occasionally. This is their third tape."

Alex tilted the cassette to read the name. "Lizard Linemen. I love these guys. I caught them at Moby Mama's last fall."

"Whoa." Sam shook his head. "It's cosmic."

"That sounds like something my sister would say," Alex said with a chuckle. "Bobo is into intergalactic forces and unseen dimensions."

"You're kidding!" Sam gasped. "Mine, too. Actually, my whole family is totally into astrology. I used to get horoscopes with my cornflakes every morning."

Alex's jaw dropped. "Amazing." She and Sam really did have a lot in common. *Why can't this work out?*

"Mind if I watch the photo shoot?" Sam asked as the elevator opened.

Alex's sense of easy companionship fizzled. He probably wanted to check out Roxanne. Or maybe Holly. Even Cedar was beginning to blossom under all the attention and glamour of the spotlight. It was only a matter of time before Sam narrowed his focus down to one of them.

"I guess not," Alex replied. "I mean, I've never really done one of these before, so I don't know whether you'd make me nervous."

Sam led the way from the elevator to a door at the end of the hall. "Hey, this stuff is a piece of cake."

Alex entered a gigantic room. Vaulted ceilings soared to almost cathedral height above her. The brick walls were covered with posters of famous bands, all looking very professional and intense.

Mixed with the posters of bands, Alex noticed quite a few fashion lay-outs, full of sleek, elegant

131

models. A tall blonde woman, comfortably dressed in chino slacks and a polo shirt, was focusing some lights against a grey muslin backdrop. When she saw Alex and Sam, she stepped forward to greet them.

"Hey, Sam." The woman smiled at Alex. "You must be Alex McQuay. Very good. I'm Nancy, and I'll be setting up your make-up and costumes."

"Make-up?"

Sam laughed beside her. "Unless you're going for the total grunge look, or working-class-hero, you have to wear make-up."

Nancy nodded. "Yeah, the cameras can make your skin look rubbery without a little covering."

They were walking towards the dressing rooms running along the left-hand wall, and Alex heard Holly's voice screech, "Oh, this is so cool!"

Nancy, Sam and Alex laughed. Alex moved to go in, but Nancy stopped her. "No, that's the girls' dressing room. Yours is along here."

Alex followed Nancy into a well-lit room comfortably furnished with a sofa and two armchairs. Along the left wall ran a dressing table with a mirrors ringed with bright lights. Alex blinked a little at the intensity even though she was still wearing her sunglasses. "Whoa, it's like megavolts in here."

Nancy motioned her to sit in a wooden chair at the make-up table. "Well, it's really important to have good lighting. Could you take off your sunglasses? We might as well get started."

Alex reluctantly took off her glasses, and caught Nancy staring at her. "You've got the most incredible eyelashes. Not fair. How come guys get the great lashes?"

She bent even closer and examined Alex's skin, making her feel like a bacteria under a microscope. "And your skin is fantastic. I don't think we'll have to use much make-up at all. What a close shave. You should model for Gillette. Here, I'll apply the make-up."

Alex shook her head. "Look, Nancy, if you don't mind, I'll do it. I've done some modelling work, actually, and I always like to apply my own make-up. I don't want the image to be too slick, you know."

Nancy gave her a sceptical look. "OK. Suit yourself. Edward may not like what you do though, so be prepared. He's really fussy."

"I'll take the risk."

"Let me just lay out the clothes we've picked out for you."

Alex swivelled in her chair to face the girl. "Listen, I don't want to be a pain, but I really think the clothes I brought should work. I'll ask Edward, of course, but the band's look is really up to us."

Nancy shrugged. "Edward should be here any minute. I'm sure he'll want to discuss it with you."

It turned out that, when Alex appeared in her new "gangster" suit, Edward loved it. Holly, Cedar and Roxanne loved it, too. The girls were decked out in baby-doll dresses with lots of frills and lots of make-up. They looked very Sixties with their big, bouffant hairstyles and long false eyelashes. Alex remembered pictures she'd seen of girl groups like the Angels and the Chiffons looking very much like the three girls looked now. They were a great contrast to her funky, dark-green striped suit.

"OK, this is what we're going for," Edward explained in his clipped voice. "Straight images of Alex, and confident, competent expressions on the girls. That way there's an equality to the impression. But the baby doll-dresses give it an altered reality. Know what I mean?"

Soon they were twisting and gyrating like they did when they played. Alex stayed in front and, while she was steaming in her suit under the hot lights, she had a feeling the shots were good.

They moved on to some close-up stills. At one

point she caught a glimpse of Sam grinning at her, pride and appreciation on his face. She decided he really must have been appreciating one of the girls. They did look incredible. Alex looked the way she always looked, like an underfed gangster.

Edward had commented on her youthful face. "You must have terrific genes. I bet you'll look twenty when you're forty. It's that Michael J. Fox effect. Great stuff."

After what seemed like hours of standing, they took a break. Edward came over to Alex. "I want to do some shots of you in just a shirt, your baggy slacks, and braces – sort of *Grapes of Wrath*. Depression era, that sort of thing. Let's lose the jacket, OK?"

"No." Under her jacket, she'd worn one of her smaller sized shirts because it had a better collar. But even with her modest proportions, anyone looking at her without her jacket would be able to see she was a girl.

Edward frowned. "Trust me, Al. It will be terrific."

Everyone stared at her. Holly chewed on her lower lip, and Roxanne, her arms crossed, merely frowned. Cedar twisted her hands together.

Sam stared at her in disbelief. "You know Edward is the best, don't you? He wouldn't suggest something that wouldn't look fantastic. I think—"

"I don't care!" Alex burst out. "Listen, I just won't. OK? Stop pushing me."

Holly gasped behind her, and suddenly Alex couldn't stand one more second of the charade. It was making her crazy. She bolted for the dressing room.

Once safe inside, she let the tears flow down her face. Alex caught sight of herself in the big mirror and gasped. Rivulets of powder streaked along her cheekbones, and she went to the sink and washed her face.

The door opened behind her.

"Go away."

"It's me, Alex."

Alex looked up from the sink to see Cedar standing there, a sympathetic look on her soft face.

"Cedar, I'm sorry. I don't know how much longer I can do this. I'm always blowing it, or about to blow it. I feel like such a jerk pretending all the time."

Cedar sat down beside her while she dried her face.

"I know it's hardest on you, Alex. But, listen, I know you did the right thing."

Alex had wiped the tears from her eyes, but they welled up again at Cedar's words.

"You do?"

Cedar nodded. "This is really going to make us big, Alex. It's what you've – what we've always wanted. I know it's not coming about quite the way you had pictured it – but the result's the same. A great gig, free publicity, and fans. Lots of them. You've always had faith in our music, Alex. And you were right." Cedar reached out and took Alex's hand, giving it a little squeeze. "I'll talk to Mr Ventriss. I'm sure he'll understand. Fix your make-up. It's OK."

Alex was floored. Quiet Cedar, who never seemed to be able to form two sentences at the same time, was going to talk to Mr Ventriss? *And here I am, the one who always knows exactly what to do next. I'm a mess.*

Alex touched up her make-up. Her face stared back at her from the mirror, pale and pathetic. Cedar hadn't closed the door the whole way, and from where she sat applying the powder to her cheeks, Alex could hear Cedar explaining how they wanted a certain look, and wasn't it their prerogative to make sure it was consistent with their overall vision of the band? Otherwise, when fans came to see them, they would feel manipulated, confused. It might seem – dishonest.

Sam and Edward reluctantly agreed. "All right," Edward said. "Let's get on with the shoot then."

Alex stared at her reflection. Her eyes were red-rimmed and teary. She couldn't go out there looking like a guy who'd been crying. Not the image they wanted for the Androgynous Zone. She quickly grabbed her sunglasses. They were beginning to be her trademark. She crammed her hat down on to her head, and flung open the door.

Time for make-believe. Again.

CHAPTER THIRTEEN

"*T*hree burgers. Hold the onions! Extra large fries."

"Order up!"

Sam had taken Alex and the girls out for an early dinner at The Cat's Pajamas, one of the best burger bars in Pike Street Market. They sat in vast red-leather booths beside floor-to-ceiling glass windows looking out on the water. Huge ferns hung from the rafters, and the wooden railings accented the rustic, casual atmosphere. Alex whistled "Fooled You" through her teeth and tried not to stare at Sam. Cooks shouted orders to each other behind the glossy chrome counter.

"So what do you guys want?" Holly asked as she studied the three-page menu. According to the lettering across the top of the menu, The Cat's Pajamas had more kinds of burgers than anywhere else in the world. Alex believed it. There were at least a hundred different varieties listed.

She pulled her gaze away from Sam and ran down the list. "How does anyone decide?"

"Well, it's my treat, so splurge," Sam declared. "You can go with the triple-decker burger bonanza with extra cheese, tomatoes, pickles, avocado, lettuce, sprouts, and bacon."

"Ugh," Roxanne groaned. "How can anyone eat all that? I think I'll stick to a plain cheeseburger."

"Dull, Roxanne. Very dull," Alex laughed.

They made their choices and, after giving the order to the waitress, fell into an awkward silence.

"So, I've got some irresistible offers for you," Sam said suddenly. Everyone looked at him, and Alex noticed that Roxanne gave him her what's-in-it-for-me? look.

"Tell us! Tell us!" Holly said eagerly, bouncing a little on the seat.

Her eyes shone, and Alex wondered, when he gave her a friendly smile, if maybe Holly wasn't the one Sam liked the best.

Alex looked at him sceptically. "You're kidding, right?"

"No, no, I'm not. And I think you guys need a manager. Someone who'll be able to keep track of your gigs and tours and bookings. And who, for a modest percentage, will help catapult you to fame and fortune." He grinned and pretended to straighten an invisible tie.

"Do you really think we need a manager?"

Cedar asked softly.

"I really do. Especially after tomorrow night."

The girls exchanged puzzled looks. Alex cocked her head to one side. "And what's tomorrow night?"

"The Battle of the Bands I entered you in," Sam said, his face all innocence.

"You *what*!!??" Alex screeched. Holly elbowed her in the ribs and Alex coughed. "Um, you what?" she asked again in her lower voice.

"Yeah, Iron Mother is hosting one of those musical free-for-alls tomorrow night. Oh, it's been scheduled for months, booked solid. But yesterday a band pulled out because one of the members got sick, so I wrote in your name and paid the entry fee."

Alex felt a sudden swirl of emotions. Part of her was eager to prove that they could be great. Part of her was terrified they weren't ready yet.

"And the winner gets a recording contract," Sam went on. "With your music, and this hot lead singer you've got, you guys are going to win. No problem."

Looking up quickly from the napkin she'd been folding, Alex felt herself grow pink. If she couldn't withstand Sam's dimple and his dark brown eyes, how was she going withstand compliments? "Uh, well, thanks, Sam. But I'm

141

not sure we're ready. I mean, we probably need to work up some new tunes, something fresh."

Sam shook his head. "Not necessary. Most bands usually stick with what's already solid – their cleanest, hottest material. I think you guys already have that in your set." He smiled across the table at her.

She felt Holly, Cedar and Roxanne watching them. "So you really think we could pull it off?" she asked quietly.

Sam nodded emphatically. "The way you wail the lyrics on 'White Noise' always gives me the most incredible sensation. And your leads. Wow. How long have you been playing guitar, anyway? About ten years or so?"

"Actually, just eight. I started when I was ten. I entered a talent show at school. You know, when students prepare the corniest stuff they can think of to impress their parents? I did a ballet number, then played the guitar and lip-synched 'Stand By—"

"Look out!" Roxanne crowed and a big blob of ketchup came squirting across the table towards Alex.

"Hey!" Alex yelled and jumped up, trying to dodge, but the stuff plopped right on her shirt. She yanked off her jacket and, stumbling out of the booth, looked in dismay at the runny ketchup stain soaking into the fabric.

"Nice going, Roxanne. What's the big idea? You did that on purpose!"

"Did not. It was a total accident. Here, I'll help you," Roxanne said, gesturing to Holly who was sitting beside her that she wanted to get out of the booth. Holly, Cedar and Sam were looking confused. "The bathrooms are over there."

Roxanne grabbed Alex's hand and dragged her towards the ladies' room. "Wait out here," she said as she disappeared inside.

It was obvious at least to Alex that Roxanne had done it on purpose. *She must be jealous,* she thought quickly. *Jealous of Sam paying attention to me. As if she didn't already have every male in Seattle drooling over her.* As Alex waited, holding the cold, soggy fabric away from her skin, she heard someone say her name. Her real name.

Luke Henderson hurried towards her.

"Where's Cody? I need to see him now."

"I don't know where he is," she snapped. "Why do you want him?"

Luke grabbed her arm roughly, and Alex tried to pull away but his fingers dug into her skin. "I just want him, that's all. Now tell me where he is."

She wrenched her arm out of his grasp. "I told you, I don't know. Back off! How did you find me, anyway?"

"I called the club. They told me about the photo session. So I went there. The assistant, Nancy or something, said you were coming here. Come on, Zan. Where is he?" Luke's eyes bored into hers.

"I already told you – I don't know."

The ladies' door opened, and Roxanne emerged with a wad of wet paper towels which she slapped against Alex's shirt.

"I saw Cody at the pier on Bainbridge this morning," Roxanne commented.

Alex shot Roxanne a furious look.

She shrugged. "Sorry. But we were on our way to get our hair done, and I noticed him."

"Thanks, Roxanne," Luke said. He flicked Roxanne's cheek with his finger, then turned to Alex again. "Tell him I need to speak to him. Today. Or else."

"Have you lost your mind, Roxanne? First you squirt me with ketchup, then you tell Luke where you saw Cody." Alex winced when the cold water on the paper towels splashed against her skin through the shirt.

"Since when are Cody's whereabouts a big secret?"

"They're not." She wasn't about to tell Roxanne that Cody was involved with Luke.

Cody would never forgive her. "Now, what's with the ketchup?"

Roxanne kept dabbing at the shirt, and the stain began to fade. Of course, Alex's shirt was completely soaked.

"You were flirting with Sam like some lovesick goon."

"I was not. We were talking business."

"Yes, you were. And you sang 'Stand By Your Man' in the fifth grade talent show, remember? Why would a ten-year old boy sing that song?"

Alex blushed. "Oh, yeah. That's right."

"And you were doing that – that *thing* you always do when you like a guy." Roxanne rubbed furiously at Alex's shirt, then chucked the stained towels in a nearby trash can.

"What thing?"

"You know exactly what I mean, Alexandra Sherwood," Roxanne said. "Every single time you fancy a guy you lean your chin in your hand and gaze longingly into his eyes. It's disgusting. You were doing it again. And, when I squirted you, you took off your coat. After making that huge deal about not taking off your coat this afternoon at the photo shoot, you rip it off in front of Sam. You could have really blown things."

Alex faced Roxanne, her pulse pounding in her veins. "You didn't have to squirt me with ketchup."

145

"I should have chucked a salt shaker at your head to knock some sense into you."

"Excuse me, Roxanne," Alex said between clenched teeth. "But you don't have to pretend every second to be someone you're not. You get to have fun, flirting, and dancing, and hanging out with guys. I have to sit there and watch. How do you think that feels?"

"You made the choice," Roxanne hissed. "Nobody's forcing you to go through with this, you know."

"That doesn't make it any easier."

"Too bad, Alex. You'll just have to get used to it. If Sam has his way, we'll end up on the cover of *Rolling Stone*. Isn't that what you wanted?" Roxanne hurried away, and Alex slumped against the door to the ladies' room.

What a mess. What a rotten mess.

And to make matters worse, Luke was combing the streets of Seattle searching for her brother.

She made her way back to the table, grabbed her jacket and slipped it on while Sam attacked his mile-high burger. She turned towards the door. "Hey, where are you going?" he asked, his mouth full.

"I – I've got to run. I forgot about some – some equipment I need to pick up."

Alex knew her excuse sounded lame, especially when Holly and Cedar were staring at her as if she'd lost her mind.

"See you guys tomorrow," Alex called. "We'll practise in the morning, OK?"

She walked to the door. A hand touched her back, and she turned to see Sam wiping his mouth with a huge napkin. "I'll come with you."

"But I have to run to catch the ferry," Alex said, easing out the door.

"I can move pretty fast," he replied with a grin. Digging into his billfold, Sam grabbed some money and gave it to Cedar. "Here, pay for the lunch with this. I'll catch you guys later."

Sam followed Alex outside and down the street. They headed south along Western Avenue, Alex walking quickly in silence. The afternoon sun dropped over the water of Puget Sound to her right, and the activity of Pike Street Market and Waterfront Park swirled round her like an invisible fabric of chaos.

More than anything in the world, she wanted to tell Sam the truth. Confess, then quit the band, go to her bedroom and pull the covers over her head for the rest of her life.

Sam strode alongside her, his hands jammed in his pockets. Finally he said, "Look, Alex, I followed you out here because I sense you're going through something right now. And I think I know what it is."

Her heart leapt. Could he know the truth, have figured it out, and not care? For half a moment she let herself hope the impossible. "Do you, really?"

"Absolutely. Things are moving fast, and you're afraid it's getting out of your control. I just want to reassure you that if you're worrying about the future of the band – don't. You guys are going to skyrocket. Already this week I got three calls from reps from record companies – biggies, too, like Columbia, Electra – who want to check you guys out. And the word's already on the street about you. The whole Seattle club scene is buzzing about Androgynous Zone."

"Thanks, Sam." Alex shoved her sunglasses up on her nose to hide her eyes and, she hoped, the way she was feeling about him.

They walked the rest of the way to the ferry terminal in silence. Alex was afraid anything she said might give her identity away.

"So you take the Winslow ferry over to Bainbridge Island, right?" Sam pointed to the large green-and-white boat moored at Pier 52. It was about to leave, and cars were lined up along the street to pull into the parking bays. This ferry would be full of commuters. The walk-on passengers would have to wait on the wide pier until they could board.

"You don't have to wait, Sam," Alex said, turning to face the water. She leaned on the rail and watched the seagulls flap overhead.

"Hey, I like waiting. I guess I've always been a people watcher. I think my ability to judge people comes from observing them closely. I can spot a fake a mile away."

"You can?"

He was staring straight into her eyes and Alex couldn't help gulping.

"Absolutely."

"Oh." Alex turned her head away from him to watch the queue of passengers. Some talked, some read the papers or books they'd brought along for the wait, some just stared at the Sound.

One man, though, Alex noticed, kept looking over at her. He was about ten people behind her, and whenever she looked away, then turned back quickly, she'd find him staring at her.

It was the man in the leather jacket. From the club. And the street.

This time he was wearing a sports coat with a polo shirt and casual slacks, as if he wanted to look like he'd just stepped out of one of those outdoor clothes catalogues so prevalent in Seattle. But it was the same man.

She gasped and turned to face Sam, who'd taken up a comfortable position leaning on the railing to her left. "Come on, Sam," she said quickly, grabbing his arm and dashing out of the queue.

"Where – what?"

She dragged him after her, and they ran across the street, heading for an alley between two warehouses.

Footsteps clattered along the cobblestones behind them, and Sam twisted to look.

"Just run!" Alex ordered.

They pounded down the alley, made a fast turn to the right and dodged between two brick buildings, where they ducked into a deep doorway. Alex's breath caught in her throat.

Sam leaned back, gasping for air. "OK, Alex," he whispered. "What's going on?"

In the distance the footsteps stopped, started, then stopped again. They pressed backwards into the doorway and stood still. Sam seemed to understand what to do without her telling him.

Finally the footsteps faded, hurrying off in the opposite direction. Alex quickly straightened her jacket and rearranged her hat, aware that Sam was staring at her.

"Are you in some kind of trouble, Alex? I mean, I don't want to pry, but since it looks like

I'm going to be your manager, I need to know everything."

Alex looked up, allowing herself one moment to look deep into Sam's eyes. What she saw there was concern and something else she couldn't quite identify. "Everything?"

Tell him now. Tell him how you tricked everyone so you could get the gig, how you've been living a lie for weeks, how you've changed your mind and want to be yourself again.

She knew she couldn't. If she did, how could he ever trust her again? And what manager wanted to deal with a band he couldn't trust? The girls would be disappointed, too. They were counting on this as their big chance. Roxanne wanted to be a star and, deep down, so did Holly and Cedar. And so did Alex.

Then there was Cody. He needed her. She didn't know exactly how he needed her, but if she did get a recording contract she would at least be able to help him repay Luke.

"No, I'm not in trouble," Alex said finally. "But that man has been following me for weeks. Everytime I turn round, it seems, there he is. On the ferry. At the club."

"The club?"

"Yeah. He was there the first night we played. I feel like he's, I don't know – stalking me."

Sam whistled softly between his teeth. Then he peered round the corner. "He's gone now. I guess we should head back to the ferry."

Alex pulled her sunglasses off to wipe the perspiration off her cheeks. Her felt hat caught on the rough brick and tumbled to the cobblestones.

Making a grab for it, her fingertips met Sam's as he bent down to retrieve the hat, too. She stopped. Together they rose in a slow movement, their eyes locked on each other.

Here I am. No hat. No sunglasses. Nothing.

Sam cocked his head to one side and held her gaze for what seemed like for ever.

Her heart pounded in her chest so hard it hurt. *He knows. He can see I'm a girl.*

But Sam just stood there, staring. Finally he handed her the hat.

Alex slammed it on to her head and slipped her glasses back on her nose.

A deep horn rang through the alley, its mournful call penetrating her foggy brain.

"That's my ferry," she cried. "Gotta run. Thanks for entering us in the contest! We'll try not to blow it."

Alex shook Sam's hand extra hard, then bolted down the alley.

CHAPTER FOURTEEN

Uranus in close aspect may bring you a sudden bolt out of the blue. Something to do with friends or popularity in general. It'll be a wake-up call from the stars that life is full of surprises. Saturn wants you to play by the rules, and Uranus amuses himself by upsetting Saturn's plans. But you're on a joyride, Aries – go for the gold.

*T*he next morning, the sound of car wheels crunching over the gravel below her window woke Alex up. She groaned, rolled over, and looked at her clock.

Six a.m. That must be Mom leaving. But she's late. She's usually out of the house by five.

Alex stumbled out of bed, grabbed her robe, and peered out the window into the fog. Mist swirled before her eyes, shrouding the trees and lane in a dismal curtain of grey.

In front of the house sat a long black car, its tinted windows rolled up. She could just about make out a man in the driver's seat, hat pulled low over his eyes, talking to someone else in the car.

Alex frowned. She backed away from the window and headed to Cody's room. Maybe he knew something about the men in the car. She opened the door to his room and peeked inside. Empty. He obviously hadn't come home again last night.

Before she could go through the list in her head of where he might possibly be, someone pounded on the front door.

Alex ran down the stairs. *That's pretty rude. It's six o'clock in the morning, and the guy can't ring the doorbell?* Her dad, whose bedroom had been moved to the ground floor, would be sure to hear the racket.

She yanked open the door and was about to chew out whoever it was, when words stuck in her throat. Two massive men in dark suits stood there, their muscles straining their coats. One had blond hair and squinty blue eyes. He stepped forward, and Alex shrank back a little.

Only one word could possibly describe them. Thugs.

She looked past them at the car. The back door sat open and inside she spotted Luke, cowering like a rabbit, his pale face a mask of fear. Dirty streaks marked his cheeks where it looked as if tears had run down his face. Tears? Luke? She couldn't believe it.

"Cody Sherwood. Where is he?" the blond asked, his voice harsh and guttural.

"Uh, I don't know. I mean, I think he stayed in town last night." Alex hoped they believed her. She didn't want them to hang round searching for Cody. They would be sure to wake up her father, and he had enough to worry about.

"I don't believe you," the man responded, taking a step towards her. She never had considered herself a coward before, but when the guy parked his powerful chest in front of her, Alex fell back another step.

The blond man glanced back at Luke, and Luke pointed upstairs towards Cody's window. Luke gave Alex a quick, terrified glance, then turned away.

The man pushed past Alex and headed up the stairs, his heavy footsteps echoing through the house. He found Cody's room, looked inside, then came back out.

Alex stood numbly as he came downstairs and, together with the other muscleman, returned to the car. Just before climbing into the car, the blond hood turned back to her and called, "You tell our boy Cody this – he can run but he can't hide."

The car drove off, leaving a thin trail of

swirling mist behind. Alex shivered and closed the door.

I've got to find Cody – before they do.

Alex raced upstairs to get dressed. As she changed into some jeans and a sweatshirt, she listened for any sign that Bobo or her dad had heard the noise. Then Alex hurried out of the house to the shed. She grabbed her bike, jumped on and pedalled off.

Following the lane to the left, she sped to the old Hillslip place. Maybe Cody was inside, hiding. It would be just like him to hide under their noses.

The house sat gloomily in the soft morning fog. As she approached, a crow cackled in the trees above her head. She flinched. *Why do crows always sound like they're laughing at you?*

Hiding the bike in some bushes near the barn, she crept silently along the side of the house. The whole area was shrouded in fog, and drops of water plink-plunked into a nearby gutter.

Alex stepped on to the front porch, checked once behind her to make sure the car wasn't anywhere nearby, and pulled open the front door, wincing when the hinges screamed.

She tiptoed into a silent, dusty hallway, the empty house closing in round her like a musty tomb. "Geez, Cody," she whispered. "Nice workplace." To the right, a stairway led upstairs, and to the left, the living room. Beyond that was the old kitchen. Boards creaked beneath her feet as she made her way to the back of the house where she'd heard Cody and Luke talking. If they had some kind of office, this was probably where it was.

But when she reached the kitchen she discovered it was empty. The counters were cracked and yellowed, the porcelain sink stained brown.

To her right were the basement steps. She plunged down them. At the bottom a door blocked the main basement from the stairs, probably to keep out the cold.

She opened it and momentarily shut her eyes.

Bright lights blinded her. *Grow lights*! Beyond where she stood marched row upon row of growing beds, bursting with plants.

"Oh, no!" she whispered. "It looks like cannabis. Acres of it."

The beds were dug neatly, and extended as far back as she could see, deep into the space beneath the house. The basement looked far bigger than normal, and as Alex moved forward, sliding through the narrow spaces between the beds, she realized the basement had been extended. Someone, Luke probably, had dug a vast room and filled it with lights and planters to produce an impressive crop of cannabis.

The moist air reeked of fertilizer, and the lights buzzed with an unworldly hum. The wires were carefully wrapped with insulating tape for extra protection from short circuits. *Definitely Cody's handiwork.*

She heard his voice in her head. "You know how many fires are started because people don't take the right precautions with wiring?"

So this is what Cody's been up to. No wonder Luke freaked when he wanted to back out. She spotted one row of lights that had burnt out, and the plants beneath it were shrivelled and thin. She could just picture Luke adding up the lost profit in his head.

"Cody?" she whispered. "Are you in here?"

She made her way steadily towards the very back of the long room, where deep shadows covered the walls.

"Cody?" Silence met her. *He must be hiding somewhere else. Better move on before—*

Thunk. Thunk. Thunk.

Footsteps!

There was someone upstairs. The steps moved across the floor and, muffled by the layers of dirt above her, were voices. More than one. Talking. Questioning.

She looked round quickly. She'd have to hide. Somewhere.

The door to the basement opened, and she retreated, trying to shrink herself into a tight ball. She felt behind her, trying to find a hole or maybe a carved-out place in the dirt wall where she could squeeze in. Her hand touched wood. A doorknob. A door?

She turned silently, felt round in the dimness. It was a door!

She pulled it open just as the door at the other end of the basement opened. Alex bolted up the rickety wooden steps and shot out into the old barn. She didn't have time to think about how Luke had managed to create a back entrance to the growing room. She just wanted to get out of there fast.

Tugging her bike from the corner where she'd left it, she jumped on and pedalled out behind the barn, heading straight across the fields where the weeds reached her chin. Bouncing roughly over the ruts, she finally reached the lane leading northward to the other end of the island.

If Cody wasn't at the Hillslip place, there was only one other place he could be. And she knew right where that was.

Her legs throbbed as she pulled into the deserted boatyard on the northeast side of the island, the sounds of the waves and screeching seabirds surrounded her.

The boatyard's days of glory were long past. Now, islanders used it for pleasure boats, and a few old-timers moored their fishing boats there. But that was all.

A dilapidated pier jutted out into the harbour on rotten piles, and Alex pedalled towards it. At the water line next to the pier rested a big dory, turned upside-down. It had been sitting there since the Forties. The paint had long since weathered off.

Underneath it, where the hollowed out part of the boat would have held fishermen and their nets, was the most perfect hiding place in the world. Cody and she had dubbed it the Fort, and it had been their special hiding place when they were kids.

Alex ditched her bike behind the main building, hurried to the dory, and crawled under the side. Her nose wrinkled at the fishy smell, and the sudden blackness made her blink.

"Cody?" she whispered. "Are you in here?"

Silence greeted her. For a moment all she could hear was the distant cry of the gulls, the water lapping a few metres away, and her own ragged breathing. To her left, where the boat sloped down towards the ground, she heard a

160

rustling and a low groan.

"Alex, is that you?" Cody's voice hissed out of the darkness.

As her eyes adjusted to the darkness, Alex could faintly make out Cody's form crawling towards her. He reached out and patted her to make sure it was really her.

"Cody, I knew you'd be here."

He curled himself into a ball, his arms hugging his long legs to his chest, and stared at her. His eyes were red-rimmed and his skin looked pastier than ever.

Alex crept closer, sitting cross-legged in front of him. "How long have you been under here?"

Cody shook his head slowly. "God, I don't know. It feels like a week. But I guess – yeah, let's see. Since yesterday, I guess. I – I had to get away from – from Luke."

A flash of fear rippled across his face.

"You're growing dope with him, aren't you?"

Cody concentrated for a moment on an ant making its miniscule way across his shoe, then he glanced up at her. There was defeat in his eyes.

"Luke came to me about three months ago and asked if I wanted to make a lot of money fast."

Alex snorted. "You should have known it would be something illegal, Cody."

Cody leaned back against the side of the boat.

"I guess I knew right from the start it wouldn't be flipping pizzas. But Mom and Dad really need money, Alex. The property taxes are due in September, you know that. And there's Dad's medical bills."

Alex sighed. There had been many nights in the last year she'd heard her parents up late, discussing their financial troubles.

"So, when he told me what I had to do, I thought it would be OK. I mean, it wasn't selling or pushing, or anything like that."

"But growing dope? You'll get thrown in prison if you're caught."

Cody pursed his lips. "But it's all underground. The heat-sensing planes can't find us."

"I know. I was just there. But what about the electricity. That must send up a red flag."

Cody nodded. "That's where I come in. Luke couldn't wire a flashlight. The wiring in that basement was pretty ancient anyway. When I rigged it, I tapped into the main power line so the usage wouldn't show up on any meters. It worked great."

"What happened?"

"I freaked out. Luke kept pushing me to set up more and more plants. The wiring is overloaded already. I got about halfway done, then I wanted out. It was just getting too scary. Every little noise felt like the marines were coming."

He shivered. The air under the boat was damp and cold, and Cody was only wearing a T-shirt and his slashed jeans.

"When I told Luke I wanted out, he went berserk. He was behind schedule. Turns out he'd borrowed the money to get started from some big-time hustler in the city. The goons came after us a week ago, saying we'd better deliver or we'd end up in the Sound."

Alex pulled her legs up to her chest. Outside, a distant ferry blew its horn. "Oh, god, Cody, how could you be so dumb? That was such a big mistake."

"So shoot me. I was just trying to help out. I – I know I haven't been doing that much, lately. This was the only thing I could think of."

"Those guys paid a visit to the house this morning," Alex said suddenly.

"What!"

"They were looking for you. Even searched the house."

"Oh, that's terrific." Cody's chin was starting to quiver. "Now what am I gonna do?"

"Call the police. That's what they're there for."

Cody stared at her. "Are you nuts? They'll arrest me."

Alex leaned forward and grabbed Cody's arm.

163

"You're going to be in far worse trouble if those hoods find you. I mean, they looked serious."

Cody shook his head. "No. I'll just have to finish the job. I'll hook up the rest of the lights, and we'll get the stupid order in a little late."

"You can't!"

"It'll be good money. If no one but you ever knows where it came from, it won't matter."

"Listen," Alex said fiercely. "If the band wins the contest tonight we'll get a recording contract. *We'll* make the money. We'll get the start we've been waiting for."

Cody held her eyes, and a flicker of hope passed through them. But then, they darkened again. "But if I go to the club, they'll find me for sure. I'll be a sitting duck."

A flash of inspiration zinged through Alex. "Not necessarily," she said with a grin.

Cody looked confused. "Alex, what are you talking about?"

Alex drummed her fingers on her chin. "I've been masquerading for weeks. There's no reason that you can't, too."

Cody shook his head. "I'm already a guy, Alex."

"Come on, Cody. Use your imagination. If we dressed you like a girl, you'd be able to get off the island, no problem."

164

"Are you crazy?" Cody shouted.

"Shh!"

"Have you lost your mind? I am not dressing as a girl. No way. Absolutely not."

"Come on, Cody, don't be an idiot. It seems to me you have two choices. Disguise yourself and get off this island, or spend the rest of your life under this boat."

Cody wavered. "I guess I could pretend I'm Dustin Hoffman in *Tootsie*."

Alex nodded. "Or Jack Lemmon and Tony Curtis in *Some Like It Hot*."

"Or Robin Williams in *Mrs Doubtfire*."

Alex was suddenly excited at the prospect of Cody experiencing a little of what she'd been going through. It was true. Misery did love company. "I'll get one of Mom's old wigs and a dress from her wardrobe. Maybe Roxanne can help with make-up."

"No! I don't want everyone to know what we're doing. Especially not Roxanne." Cody rubbed a hand over his face in anguish. "She'd never let me forget it."

Alex shrugged. "OK, OK. She doesn't have to do your make-up but we do have to tell the band. Because my plan involves them."

Something bumped the boat, and she and Cody jumped. They stared at each other. Her heart felt like it was stuck in her throat. *Oh no! I led them right to Cody. I'll never forgive myself.*

"Hey, are you guys in there?" came a soft voice from outside. Then a slim figure slithered into the narrow gap between the boat railing and the ground.

"Bobo?" Cody asked. "What are you doing here?"

Bobo grinned. "I wondered where Alex went this morning. I was half awake when that black car showed up. I heard someone walking down the stairs, then I looked out the window and saw this big black car disappear in the mist." She looked at her brother, and gulped, "I – I thought they took you away."

Cody leaned forward and put his arm round her slender shoulders. "Nah. I'm too clever for them. And now your brilliant sister has come up with a ridiculous plan for getting me off the island."

Bobo smiled. "Another disguise?"

"How did you know?" Alex said, laughing quietly.

"Just psychic, I guess. What can I do?"

Together they decided that Bobo and Alex would head back to the house to get what they needed for Cody's disguise.

"But what about when we get to the club?"

Cody said. "How am I going to set your levels and do sound tech stuff dressed like a girl? This isn't going to work."

Alex chewed the tip of her finger. "Bobo might be able to help us there. I've got a plan. I just need to work out the details in my head. Right now I'll go and get you some food, Cody. We'll meet back here in an hour. And then I'll explain it."

Cody shivered. "I hope you know what you're doing, Alex. If not, I might as well head for the North Pole."

"Don't worry." Alex gave her brother a hug. "'Fooled You' has become my theme song."

CHAPTER FIFTEEN

Alex stared at her brother from her seat on the opposite side of the ferry deck. Cody stared back, his brown eyes smouldering in irritation. Alex shook her head. *Funny. Make-up makes him look angry.*

Cody looked away, pulling at the dress Alex had found for him, an old, baggy, floral one, shaped rather like a sack. In their mother's brown wig, a little make-up, and a loose sweater, he looked like a middle-aged woman who had seen better days.

The rest of the band was sitting with Alex at one of the big booths by the windows. They'd agreed to the plan, too. Reluctantly. But they were so nervous about the Battle of the Bands that, if Cody wanted to hang out with them dressed as a girl, it couldn't possibly make them any more uncomfortable.

"I couldn't eat all day," Cedar was saying. "I thought I couldn't possibly get any more keyed up than I was an hour ago. And I am. More nervous,

I mean."

"Just wait. Wait till you see the crowds," Holly said. She took a long gulp of fruit juice.

Cedar gave her sister a worried look. "That really makes me feel better."

Holly patted Cedar on the shoulder. "Glad to help."

"Listen, you guys," Alex said. "Are you all set on the plan? Roxanne? You're awfully quiet. I haven't heard more than three completely defeatist statements from you. Are you feeling OK?"

Roxanne, who'd been eyeing Cody again, shook her head. "I'm OK. Cody just looks so ridiculous. What is it about guys dressed like girls that is so outrageous? I mean, girls wear men's clothes all the time, and it looks fine." She stopped and stared at Alex. "You know, Alex, when you came up with this idea to pass as a boy, I thought you'd lost your mind. I mean, who'd have thought it would've worked?"

"I think it even suprised me," Alex confessed.

Roxanne smiled. "I just want you to know that, regardless of what happens tonight, you were right." Roxanne turned to the others. "Did you get that? I, Roxanne Flint, being of sound mind and body, fully admit that Alexandra Sherwood was right."

Holly shook her head. "Boy, I wish I had a tape recorder for this moment."

"I think a simple signed statement will do," Alex joked. She turned to Roxanne and, still keeping up her boy disguise, stuck out her hand. "Rox, thanks. You don't know how much that means to me."

They laughed. Roxanne drummed on the table with her spoon and fork, but stopped suddenly and glanced towards the main door of the cafeteria. "Uh-oh. Look out, Alex."

"What?" Alex turned to see Candy Rapper heading straight for them like a guided missile. "Oh no! This is not what I need."

"Hi!" The blonde grinned down at them, her perky smile in place. "I hoped you'd be on this boat. Are you heading for Iron Mother?"

Roxanne bit her cheek. Holly stared into her glass. Cedar peered out the window as if she'd suddenly developed a passion for marine biology.

"Uh, yeah. We're doing the Battle of the Bands."

"Wow! That is so cool. Can I join you? I mean, I'd love to tell my friends I hung out with you before you got discovered."

Candy didn't wait for permission, but squeezed herself into the booth beside Alex. Her thigh pressed against Alex's leg, and Alex slid

170

closer to Holly.

"I know you guys will win. I mean, no one else has your sound. It's fresh."

Everyone nodded and made feeble attempts to smile.

Alex felt like crawling under the table.

"So, Alex, is your brother running the sound board again?" Candy asked. "He's really good."

A heavy silence descended on the table.

"Uh, yeah. He's really good, all right. But he's sick. We have to use a club technician tonight."

"Oh, too bad! I know you'll miss him. I mean, the mix on 'Illusion Lightning' is totally underground. Heavy and hot. Too bad your brother won't be doing it."

Alex nodded. "Yeah, it is."

It felt like Candy was giving Alex the third degree. "Does Cody hang out in the city much?" Candy asked, picking up a fork and twirling it like a baton.

I bet she was a cheerleader in high school.

"Not really. We're pretty busy on the island."

"You have a farm, right?"

Alex clenched her jaw. How could Candy know that? And if she knew that, what else did she know? Something felt very wrong about her. Suddenly Alex felt an overwhelming desire to put as much distance as possible between them.

"Well, I'm not sure you could call it a farm any more. It's more like a lot of land covered with weeds. Excuse me, Candy." Alex dislodged herself from the booth and smiled at the group. "I'll be back in a minute."

Alex headed for the corridor where the restrooms were located but veered off and took a side door into the staff lounge. She wasn't about to sit out there and get interrogated by some groupie.

Cody had seen her escape from the booth and followed her into the lounge. Up close, he really did look funny, with the blusher streaked across his cheeks and the faint line of eyeliner accenting his brown eyes. Alex pressed her lips together so she wouldn't smile.

"Oh, go ahead," he said ruefully. "You might as well laugh. Everybody else is getting a good yuck at me in this outfit. I saw Roxanne out there trying not to collapse."

"It's amazing," Alex said. "But in that outfit, you look like Aunt Louise. Maybe we should pretend that you're her. I mean when you're hiding backstage, manning the sound board."

"Fine. Say anything you want." He dropped into a chair and checked his watch. "Ten more minutes and we'll be docking."

"You're sure you know what you're supposed

to do?" Alex tried not to let the worry show on her face. This was her idea, after all. There was also a big possibility that the whole thing could blow up in their faces.

Don't think about that now. Think about the music. Keep cool. Keep calm. Everything will work out.

A door leading from the other end of the ferry opened behind them and a figure dressed in blue jeans, flannel shirt and faded blue baseball hat stepped inside.

Alex stood up. "You ready?"

Bobo nodded and grinned. "As ready as I'll ever be."

Alex went over the plan once more, re-emphasizing, "As soon as we hit the club, Bobo, you drop into the pit at stage right. Stay there until it's our turn. Don't talk to anyone and don't turn round."

Bobo gave her a thumbs-up. "For the next four hours, I'm Cody. Silent Cody."

Cody pursed his lips. "Be careful, baby sister. If anything bad happens, drop the disguise, immediately."

Bobo held up her right hand. "I promise."

They agreed that once the ferry docked, Bobo, in her Cody disguise, would walk with the band. Cody, as Aunt Louise, promised to hang back,

173

making sure to separate himself from the band. But Alex would stay by the stage door and let him in a few minutes after the rest of the group.

Above their heads, the ferry's deep horn echoed through the night, signalling that they were about to dock. Bobo, Alex and Cody exchanged looks. Alex had a feeling they were never going to be the same after this night.

Twenty minutes later, the group was standing outside Iron Mother. From inside came the wail of a guitar as the band onstage kicked in with an elaborate lick. There was an answering roar from the crowd inside.

Roxanne paused at the steps leading to the stage door. "Whoever they are, they're good," she said.

"We're better," Alex said simply as she led them down the concrete steps. There was a group of people clustered round the door, and Alex suddenly caught sight of the man in the suit. He was standing a short distance from the group – staring at her.

She froze.

There he is again! Why? Why did this guy seem to be everywhere? No matter where she went, this guy was there. There was no reason for him to be following her.

Or was there?

Suddenly, she knew. *Cody.* He was after Cody. *He's some kind of hit man.*

"Oh, god," she whispered, biting her lip. Cody would be passing this man in a few short minutes. Alex crossed her fingers. *Please let his disguise work.*

Before she could decide what to do, someone yelled, "It's them! Androgynous Zone!"

Suddenly a crowd of fans mobbed them in a screaming mass of adoration. They tugged at their clothes and grabbed their hands.

Alex was thrust against the wall, and Roxanne almost fell off the stairs.

"Get through them!" Alex screamed. They pressed forward against the tide of people, and slowly forced their way to the door. Alex made a dive for the door, held it open just long enough for Cedar, Holly, Roxanne and Bobo to get through, and then yanked it shut.

"Hey, someone help!" she shouted.

From behind her, a hand reached forward and slid the heavy bolt in place. There was a howl of protest from outside, then silence.

"The price of fame," a comforting voice sounded in her ear.

She turned and smiled with relief at Sam. Beyond him, throngs of technicians milled about the backstage area. Several waiting bands talking

175

among themselves, some thumbed their guitars softly, others paced. A few just stood and stared.

"A small price," Alex repeated, trying to sound unperturbed. She tried to slow her heartbeat down by taking slow, deep breaths.

Out on stage, the announcer shouted the name of the group that had just finished. "Let's hear it for Joystick!"

The crowd cheered. A nauseous feeling crept into Alex's stomach. It was clear the house was pumped about the previous band.

"Don't worry about it," Sam said as if he'd read her mind. "They're just being polite."

Alex smiled, trying to make it look like a smirk. "I hope they're as polite to us."

Sam laid his hand on her shoulder, letting it rest there for a long moment. "Oh, they'll do more than be polite. You'll see."

A small knock sounded on the stage door. Alex turned, explaining, "That's my Aunt Louise. I told her to come to the stage door and I'd let her in."

Sam slid open the bolt and a disguised Cody squeezed inside. "They're animals out there!" he exclaimed, forgetting to alter his deep voice.

Sam's eyes widened in surprise but he didn't have a chance to react because just then Alex gasped, "Oh, my god, he's backstage."

She pointed to the man in the suit who had

been following her. His eyes were fixed on all of them.

Suddenly the loudspeaker boomed backstage.

"We're going to take a short intermission but don't go away. Our next entry in Iron Mother's Battle of the Bands is that hot new group – Androgynous Zone!"

CHAPTER SIXTEEN

"Illusion lightning,
Casting its light on what could be;
Isn't it fright'ning?
'Cause that laser cuts to the heart of me."

Alex's voice slid under Holly and Cedar's harmonies, and together they let loose.

Her guitar felt light, almost as if it had become part of her body, and her fingers rippled across the strings. Effortless. Automatic.

On one side of the stage stood the man in the suit, who'd retreated the moment the band took the stage.

On the other side Candy Rapper bounced to the music, waving and smiling. Only three metres away from her, Cody, still dressed to look like Aunt Louise, mixed the sound and adjusted settings from behind a black curtain. Every song had been perfect.

The crowd was loving every minute of it. Gyrating bodies fused into a mass of movement and colour, and when Alex blasted into the final chorus everyone started screaming.

As the song ended, Alex sensed movement across the stage near where the man in the suit had been. She glanced over, blinking sweat out of her eyes.

Luke Henderson stood there, pale and looking frightened. Behind him loomed the two thugs who'd come to her house the day before.

Alex wailed the last line and the crowd erupted.

This is the end. Cody will be arrested. Or taken away by those hit men. Me, too, probably.

The crowd kept shouting, the building vibrating with the noise of hundreds of voices chanting, "More! More! More!"

They ran offstage. Roxanne shrieked with joy. "They loved us! They loved us!"

The chanting continued, and the announcer ran to them, gesturing madly. "Get back out there before they tear the place apart."

"Roxanne," Alex said, grabbing her arm. "Get them dancing while I get Cody out of here."

Roxanne's mouth dropped open. "Without our lead singer? Are you nuts?"

"I've never been so serious in my entire life," Alex replied. "Now, please – get out there."

Roxanne led the girls back on stage and

counted them into a trio version of "Sin", which they'd been working on for weeks.

Alex dashed behind the curtain where Cody was hiding. His face was covered with sweat, and the dress hung in damp folds across his lean chest.

"Here," Alex said, wriggling out of her suit and handing the clothes to Cody. Underneath, she wore bike shorts and a shiny blue halter top. Regular girl clothes. They felt great, even though she'd been cooking in them all evening under her suit.

"Put on this suit," she ordered. "And get out there. Pretend you're me. Take a bow after 'Sin'."

Cody stared at her. "Why? What's happened?"

"Luke's here."

"Oh, god."

"And his buddies. They're over on stage left."

Cody ripped the dress off, quickly climbed into the suit Alex had worn, and used the dress to wipe the make-up off his face. He chucked the wig in the corner and slipped Alex's sunglasses on to his nose.

"After the bow, lead the band out of the front door," Alex instructed. "And when you reach the street – run. To the nearest police station."

Cody grabbed his sister's hands. "You're a good kid, Alex. I've never told you that, but you are."

Tears stung her eyes. "Cody, this is a chance for a fresh start. Take it." She plunked her felt hat on to her brother's head. "Be careful."

As Alex pushed Cody on to the stage, she was vaguely aware of Candy Rapper standing off to their left. She'd apparently witnessed the whole exchange. But Alex didn't care. All that mattered was that Cody made it out of the building safely.

Alex looked for Luke and the two men. They were doing exactly what she expected them to be doing – staring at the pit. Staring at Bobo, dressed in Cody's blue plaid flannel shirt, a baseball cap pulled low over her eyes. She was pretending to adjust some knobs on a fake sound board, and when she looked up Alex gave her a quick signal from the wings.

"Get ready," she mouthed.

Bobo nodded.

The song finished, and the audience screamed and screamed. Cody grabbed Holly and Cedar's hands, then the four of them leapt from the stage, threading their way through the tightly packed crowd.

Pandemonium broke loose as the dancers realized the band had come to them. Suddenly, Luke bolted across the stage and jumped into the pit.

Alex raced after him, arriving just as Luke

ripped off Bobo's baseball hat.

"Leave my sister alone, Luke," Alex cried.

Luke shoved Alex, and she almost fell. A hand steadied her, then a forceful voice barked, "Hold it right there, Luke Henderson."

Alex wheeled round and was stunned with astonishment.

Candy Rapper stood in the pit, shoulders back, a fierce expression on her usually smiling face. She held a small leather case in her hand. It flipped open to reveal a badge and a photo ID card with the words "Drug Enforcement Agency" lettered across the top.

"Oh, man," Luke moaned. "A narc."

"You have the right to remain silent." Candy began reading Luke his rights as she clapped handcuffs on him.

There was a sudden commotion at the front door of the club, and Alex craned her head to see. The two thugs, once they saw that Luke had been arrested, made a beeline for the exit. But they were stopped at the door by the man in the leather jacket. He was a policeman, not a hit man!

Alex stared at Candy Rapper. She seemed too young and outrageous to be a cop. "Don't worry, Alex," Candy said. "If your brother turns State's evidence, and testifies against this slime and his pals, he'll get off with a pretty light sentence."

Bobo's mouth was hanging open. "You're a police officer?"

Candy nodded. "Narcotics. Special Assignment. And believe it or not, my name really is Candy Rapper. My mom does have a twisted sense of humour." She winked at Bobo, nodded once to Alex, then led Luke out.

Cody, who was taken away with Luke and the others, paused at the door and gave Alex a wave. For the first time in months he looked happy.

It all happened so fast that no one in the club seemed to even know the police had been there. The announcer confirmed it when he stepped up to the microphone and announced, "Yo, people! The judges have made their decision."

The crowd quietened. At the back, Holly, Cedar and Roxanne held hands and faced the stage.

Alex was still in the pit with Bobo. As she waited for the announcement she was certain that her heart had stopped beating. Time had stopped. There was no yesterday or tomorrow. Just this moment.

"You all know what the winners get," the man said. "A Force One recording contract. That's right. The hottest, most successful studio in Seattle will be recording the winner of tonight's battle. Do you want to know who that winner is?"

"Yes!" screamed the crowd.

"Yes," whispered Alex. Beside her, Bobo clutched her hand and gave it a squeeze.

The announcer slowly opened the slip of paper in his hand. His eyes widened. He paused. Everyone held their breath.

"The recording contract goes – in a unanimous decision, I might add – to Androgynous Zone!"

The place exploded with screams. Holly, Cedar and Roxanne raced for the stage. Alex moved to join them when Bobo pulled her back.

"Zan," she hissed. "You're not in the right clothes. You look like a girl."

Alex looked down at her outfit and gasped. "Oh, my god. What do I do?"

The announcer had now put his hand to his eyes and was squinting into the audience. "Will Alex McQuay please come forward."

Now Sam had joined the group on the stage.

The audience started chanting, "We want Alex. We want Alex."

Bobo squeezed her hand. "This is your moment. Uranus has brought that sudden bolt out of the blue. Change it now or forever hold your peace."

Alex squeezed her sister's hand. "Here goes. Wish me luck." She took a deep breath and joined the rest of the band on the stage.

The chanting petered out as the shocked realization rippled through the crowd. "Alex is a girl!"

Sam stared at her in amazement. Then he stepped stiffly forward and held out a document. It was a signed and notarized contract with Force One Recording.

"Uh, here, Alex," Sam said, not looking her in the eye. "Here is your prize."

There it was. A contract. In her hand.

And Sam wouldn't look at her.

Alex stepped up to the microphone, facing the hushed crowd. "I am Alexandra McQuay Sherwood. Yes, I am a girl and yes, we did lie to you."

A couple of people booed.

"Wait a second." Alexandra raised her hand. "Before you decide that what we did was totally wrong, I'd like to tell you why we did it. We auditioned for some clubs here in town. And you've heard us. We're pretty good. Aren't we?"

There was a long moment of silence. Then some of the crowd applauded politely. But nobody cheered.

"This is a funny business. Some people look at an all-girl band and think, oh, we've heard you before. You're the same as every other all-girl band in Seattle or New York or LA."

A few girls in the audience made noises of agreement.

"But we don't see ourselves as four girls. We're musicians. That's what we do. Play music. That's what defines us. We're no different from any other band. All we want is to be judged on our musical talent. All we wanted was a chance to be heard."

The complaining faded a little, and the "all right" and "way cool" comments grew louder.

"I want to thank you for giving us this chance. Maybe it's our only one. Maybe you won't want to hear us after this."

There was a shout from the back, "No way!"

"But thank you." The tears that had been threatening to come welled over and Alexandra quickly ran offstage.

She knew the crowd would never forgive her for pretending to be something she wasn't. And neither would Sam.

I'm a fool. A total fool!

She had just ruined her big break. The chance for all of them – Roxanne, Cedar and Holly – to break through to success. *They hate me. And I don't blame them.*

The crowd backstage parted as she ran past. She ran out the stage door, shivering as the cool night air raised goosebumps on her hot skin.

Alexandra hurtled down the street towards the darkened pier, her footsteps thudding along the planks. She ran right to the end, then stopped. Her tears splashed over the railing into the water.

Beyond her, the moonlight blazed a silver trail across the waves. Alexandra had always loved the moon path. She used to think it was telling her to follow it and she'd have whatever she wanted.

Now it mocked her.

You've ruined your one and only chance to be something special, to be great.

"Hey, Alexandra," a voice whispered from behind her.

She wiped her eyes but didn't turn round.

Sam joined her at the railing. He stood staring at the water. Then he turned slightly and she sensed his smile.

"The crowd went berserk after you left."

She gulped. "They're angry, aren't they? Do you have to refund their money? I guess the runners-up can have our contract."

Sam put his hands on her shoulders and held her away from him, his face filled with amazement. "Are you kidding? They want you back. They love you. Holly, Roxanne and Cedar got lifted over the heads of the crowd and passed round the room. Quite an honour."

"You're not serious." She searched his face.

"Of course I am. You thought they were upset?"

Alexandra nodded. It was the first time she could really gaze into Sam's eyes. And as always she could feel the electricity charge through her bloodstream.

"That crowd is on your side. I couldn't have planned a better publicity stunt if I'd tried."

"Stunt?" Alexandra put her hands on her hips. "That was no stunt."

"Who cares?" Sam chuckled, pushing her short hair away from her face. "It worked. And Cliff Barker was blown away when you came out as a girl. He almost fainted. Now he wants to buy out your contract."

Alexandra threw her hands in the air. "I can't believe it! Barker's the one who started this thing. He's the reason we did this whole masquerade."

Sam laughed. "Well, don't tell him that. He'll want a cut. I'm not surprised, though. He never could see what was right in front of his nose." He chuckled again, the dimple appearing in his cheek. "I guess there's a lot of that going round."

Alexandra studied Sam's face. "You're not angry?"

"You're kidding. This whole situation has been driving me crazy. I haven't been able to sleep at night. All I've done is think about you. I thought

– well, you know what I thought. Let me tell you, it was giving me a serious identity crisis."

"I'm sorry, Sam. You must be disappointed." She remembered the admiring looks he'd given Holly and Roxanne.

"No, I'm not disappointed," he whispered.

"And you still want to represent me?"

"Represent you? I want to date you! No, that's not what I mean – well, yes it is. I want to spend time with you. To be with you." He flushed, looked away, then looked back at her. "What I mean is – I want to be part of your life, Alexandra Sherwood. A big part of your life."

Alexandra was about to say, "Me too," but Sam's lips pressed against hers and all she could do was murmur, "Mmmm".

Over Alexandra's shoulder, the moon path shimmered, settling into a clear, straight path to the future.

ZODIAC

*ARIES*TAURUS*GEMINI*CANCER*LEO*VIRGO*LIBRA*
*SCORPIO*SAGITTARIUS*CAPRICORN*AQUARIUS*PISCES*

Twelve signs of the Zodiac. Twelve novels, each one embracing the characteristics of a zodiac sign. Pushed to the extreme, these characteristics lead down twisting paths into tales of mystery, horror, romance and fantasy.

Whatever your sun sign, you will want to read Zodiac, the series written in the stars.

SERIES CREATED BY JAHNNA N. MALCOLM

GEMINI:
SENSITIVE, UNPREDICTABLE
MIRROR IMAGE

*G*abrielle is desperate; her behaviour erratic. Someone is tormenting her, or is it her imagination? Is she the victim of a split personality or is a ghost from the past driving her insane?

LEO:
DRAMATIC, LOVES THE SPOTLIGHT
STAGE FRIGHT

*L*ydia loves to perform. As an actress she's the best and she knows it! But her confidence is shaken when a series of accidents disrupt her life... First her home is robbed, then she's almost run over by a car. Somebody wants to hurt Lydia, is it someone jealous of her success - someone driven by an urge beyond their control?

AQUARIUS:
INDEPENDENT, INNOVATIVE
SECOND SIGHT

Amber has always been different. She discovers that she has had special powers since she was a little girl. But these powers frighten her especially when her dreams about other people start to come true - sometimes with dramatic results. If only she could use these powers to really help people… instead of creating havoc and fear.

PISCES:
A DREAMER, KNOWS SECRETS
SIXTH SENSE

Phoebe is a loner. She can sense when something's wrong, but people distrust her and are afraid of her premonitions. When Mark Chenier disappears, images grow in Phoebe's mind – she knows where Mark is, but no one, except her Cajun grandmother, believes her. Can she prove that she is right and that her 'dreams' really tell the truth?